ONCE IN A BLUE MOON

KRISTAN HIGGINS

ONCE IN A BLUE MOON by Kristan Higgins

A novel

Copyright © 2026 by Kristan Higgins

ISBN:

Cover design by MiblArt

Interior book design by Mel Jolly, AuthorRx

Published by Kristan Higgins. For a complete list of Kristan's books, including others in the Wellfleet series, visit www.kristanhiggins.com.

Audiobook published by Recorded Books

Printed in the United States of America.

❋ Formatted with Vellum

This book is dedicated to you, dear reader. Thank you for your love of stories, and for spending some time with mine.

ONE

WINNIE

Windsor Eleanora Smith was not a homewrecking whore. It's just what everyone was saying these days. Including her brother.

"Wear it with pride," said Robbie, younger by three and a half years physically and two decades emotionally. Winnie held up his gift, a white sweater with the letter A embroidered in red, front and center. "Not funny," she said. Still... "Where did you get it?"

"Special order," said Rosie, his fiancée. "We debated with going for a Coldplay kiss-cam meme, but this is more classic. And I agree. It will really screw with the gossips."

It was yet another Smith Family dinner. They'd assembled at her sister Addison's house—Winnie's parents, Grandpop, her four siblings, their partners and three nieces —a mob, in other words. Ostensibly, they were there to discuss Robbie and Rosie's wedding in a few months. Given recent events, however, they were also keen on showing support for Winnie, the recently crowned homewrecker, who had only wrecked one home, and not even on purpose.

"I kind of love it," she said, giving Robbie a nod of

thanks. Once, they had shared a bedroom, while she did not share his sense of humor, she appreciated that he'd given some thought to her dilemma.

That being said, this dinner was killing her. She hated being the center of attention—her family was way too big and growing every year. The noise was like the ocean...constant and huge. But they were hers, she supposed. Grandpop, aka Robert Smith, beloved by all; her parents, Gerald and Ellie; her siblings—Harlow, the oldest, married to Grady, mother to Matthew, stepmother to Luna; Addison, the older-by-three-minutes identical twin, her unsmiling wife Nicole, and their two demon-daughters, Esme and Imogen; Lark, the other, more perfect twin and her new husband, Dante, also perfect (Boston firefighter, utterly gorgeous in body and spirit); and Robbie, the only boy, the scene stealer, adored, doted on, somehow engaged to Rosie, Harlow's best friend from college and therefore older than Robbie by ten years. They were getting married in December, and Winnie had offered to be their wedding planner...Rosie's father was an entertainment attorney in Los Angeles and insisted on paying her a Hollywood wage. Thank God, because she'd need the money. Until this week, Winnie had owned a fairly lucrative event planning business. As of three days ago, it was a dumpster fire.

"This will pass, honey," Lark said. "Someone else's crisis will come up, and people will move on. Life in a small town, you know?" She reached across Dante and squeezed Winnie's hand.

"Thanks." She forced a smile at her sister.

"More wine?" asked Harlow, the other perfect sister, holding the bottle over Winnie's glass.

"Keep it coming," Winnie said. She didn't drink very often, but this week called for it.

"You didn't *know* you were sleeping with another woman's husband," Mom said, stating the obvious. "*He's* the liar. People should cut you some slack."

"We cannot help with whom we fall in love," Grandpop said kindly. "He was using a different name! Who can blame you for not knowing his true identity?"

"The Mommy Mafia is who," Winnie said. "My client base, in other words."

"When I think of the 'other woman,'" Robbie said, making air quotes, "I picture someone more like my beautiful fiancée here. Not you, Winnebago. No offense to either of you, of course."

"I'm flattered," Rosie said, kissing his cheek.

"*I'm* not," Winnie said. "Seventeen parties canceled this week alone. Wives, lock away your husbands, because Winnie Smith is arranging your kids' First Communion party, and she's an immoral slut." It was possible that she was buzzed, and more power to it.

"Oh, honey. Don't call yourself that," Dad said. "You're wonderful. The most moral person I know."

"Yeah, you're not quite there yet," Robbie said. "You can be an aspirational slut. Don't get ahead of yourself. I had to put in years for that title." Rosie laughed and tilted her head against his shoulder.

"Can you two not be so...happy?" Winnie asked.

"Unfortunately, Winnie's right," Addison said, checking her phone. She couldn't go thirty seconds without looking at it. "People *are* blaming her. A few vague-book posts, a sudden burst of shitty reviews on Yelp. A text chain that went on for miles before they realized I was on it. So yeah, everyone *is* hating on her. They're also saying Tanner is an asshole. But mostly that Winnie should've done better research, and who doesn't know these things in this day and age."

"You know, Addie, sometimes saying nothing works, too," Harlow said.

"What?" Addison said. "I defend her! Obviously. Plus, information is power."

"Addie is the queen of the Mommy Mafia," Nicole, her wife, said proudly. "Girls! Stop eating the cheese spread with your hands."

"Sleep around and live life to the fullest," Robbie advised sagely. "I did, and now I'm engaged to the most perfect woman in the world."

"Robbie, shut up," Harlow said, smacking him upside the head. "Honestly, Rosie, are you sure you want to marry this little dweeb?"

"Weirdly, I am," Rosie said. "He's loved me since he had hormones. Who can resist that? And *we* won't fire you, Winnie. You're still our wedding planner, and my father wants to spare no expense for his beloved and only child."

"Thanks," Winnie muttered, polishing off her wine. *Only child.* Lucky. And while she was grateful to Mr. Wolfe for saying "unlimited budget," it's not like it was a long-term solution. Her event planning business had always been more focused on the more commonplace celebrations in a person's life. Birthdays, anniversaries, family reunions. Baby showers and gender reveals (though she thought they were tempting fate and a bit self-aggrandizing). There were plenty of other event planners who fed off the stress and fanfare of the zillion-dollar weddings and bat and bar mitz-vahs, the demanding clients and expensive vendors. Winnie had always tried to focus on the regular people. For exam-ple, a five-year-old's birthday party.

But Wellfleet, Massachusetts, like most of the towns on

the outermost part of Cape Cod, was small. Tiny in the off-season, especially in terms of the year-round families who made up the bulk of her business. Life on Cape Cod was expensive, housing prices were ridiculous, and Winnie had just lost her base. Life in a small town, as Lark said, meant it took mere minutes to cancel a business. Or a person.

"Mommy? Mommy? Mommy?" Esme chanted. "Can Luna sleep over? Mommy? Mommy? Can she? Can she?"

"Mama, can she? Please? Please? Can she? We'll be good! I promise! We will be!" Imogen said. She would never need a bullhorn, no sir.

"Daddy, can I sleep over? Please? Please? Can I?" Luna added.

Amazing that people *wanted* children. Winnie liked having nieces and a nephew, but this? All day, every day? The world was crowded enough, and bless her sisters for procreating so her parents had grandchildren, releasing Winnie from any guilt they might try on her.

"Yes, yes, fine," Addie said. "Of course. Luna, we love having you. Find something to do, though. The grownups are talking about your aunt Winnie and her problems."

"What problems?" Esme asked. "Did you do something bad, Aunt Winnie? What was it? Did you kill someone?"

"I'll never tell," Winnie said. "My glass is empty, by the way." Grady obliged with a gentle smile. Her favorite brother-in-law. Had Dante poured the wine, he would've nabbed the title, but the night was Grady's.

"You did. You killed someone," Esme said. "You're so fun, Aunt Winnie."

"I really am."

"Don't encourage her, Winnie," Nicole snapped. "Girls, killing people is wrong. Go watch a movie." The children obeyed, but Imogen first lowered her head and took a massive bite of cake, no hands. The kid grinned up at her, and Winnie gave a slight nod of approval before Nicole herded them off.

"Winnie, my dear, we all know who you are," Grandpop said. "And we love and support you."

"Thanks, Grandpop." She felt the unfamiliar sting of tears and ordered them not to fall. She hadn't cried since she was eight, and she wasn't about to start now.

"We're all still going to trivia night, right?" Harlow said. "Semifinals." Harlow took her trivia team way too seriously.

"Of course I'm going. I'm the DJ," said Robbie. "The most important person there."

"Come with us, Winnie," said Lark. "It'll be good for you to get out. Dante and I are coming, too."

"We'll make sure you have fun," Dante said. "And if anything happens, we're your bodyguards, how's that?"

Fun brought forth images of a cozy house in Antarctica, with only penguins for neighbors. Winnie wouldn't have to talk to anyone, just ice fish, keep a fire going and focus on not freezing to death. Better than the pointed stares and whispers and hostile mutters she'd encountered these past few days. You'd think society would be past that—how many politicians had blatantly cheated on their spouses? How many actors? It didn't hurt their careers, did it? But here in Puritanical Massachusetts, it seemed like women were still blamed for husbands who couldn't keep it in their pants.

"Please come," Rosie said.

Winnie hesitated. She wanted to crawl into bed and rewatch *The Office* for the nineteenth time and doomscroll. But she knew better. She was heartbroken (and a little drunk), and if she went home, she'd almost definitely curl into a ball and cry. Being with her family was probably the safer option. "Sure," she said. This way, she could also avoid seeing how many more clients had canceled.

And face the fact that Mitchell—i.e., Tanner Johnson—hadn't reached out. Mitchell, the first man who'd ever said he loved her, outside of Dad and Grandpop. The only man Winnie had ever loved.

"I *love* trivia night!" said Grandpop, who was on Harlow's team. "But we should stay and help Addie and Nicole clean up. You lovely girls are such *wonderful* hostesses! I ate thirteen of those little water chestnuts wrapped in bacon. My favorite!"

"Please don't stay," Nicole said bluntly. "I'd rather clean up on my own."

"We'll give the girls their baths and tuck-ins, how's that?" Mom suggested.

And so off they went...Grandpop, Harlow and Grady, Lark and Dante, Robbie and Rosie...and Winnie, the other Smith kid.

Harlow was a pillar of the town, the oldest, the smart one who got full scholarships for college and law school. She now ran Open Book, a bustling indie bookstore, with Grandpop. Addison, one of the stunningly beautiful identical twins, had "married well" and was now one of those irritating mommy influencers, showing off her beautiful daughters, beautiful home and beautiful wife. Lark, the other stunningly beautiful twin, was a doctor who had recently married a Boston firefighter. She was the kindest soul in the universe and everyone's favorite (Winnie's, too). Robbie was the baby of the family, spoiled since Mom first pushed him into the world. He was The Boy, carrier of the Smith family surname, named after Grandpop and now marrying Rosie, Harlow's best friend from college.

And then there was Winnie. The other one. The one

whose name people couldn't remember (Robbie made a sport out of it), the not-beautiful, not-brilliant sister who, until she became the aforementioned home-wrecking whore, had pretty much blended into the background. "Oh, you're one of the Smiths? The bookstore sister? The one with the big house on Lieutenant Island? The doctor? No? I guess I didn't know there were four girls."

But in the past few years, she'd busted her ass as an event planner. It was a great job for someone who liked to be in the background, who put in countless hours to create the best event for a small budget, who would make something beautiful and fun and touching and also set up thirty tables and serve drinks if the bartender didn't show. It wasn't like it had been her particular calling, but she'd done some seasonal work for an established event planner for a few years, was organized and hard-working. Jobs were hard to find, and when her boss moved to France, Winnie did her best to fill the niche. Now that career was over. Robbie and Rosie's wedding would stave off the bills for a little while, but she'd either have to rebound or find something else to do.

All because she'd fallen in love with a rat bastard, lying, cheating asshole chef.

Last week, Nycholiss (as in Nicholas) Johnson turned five, an event Winnie had organized—dinosaur bounce house, dinosaur cake, dinosaur party favors, dinosaur games. Fifty guests, most of them adults, with a dozen or so kids under the age of ten—friends, classmates, cousins, as well as younger sisters Bruklynne (as in New York) and Kaedeigh (as in Katie). Blakelee, the mother of the birthday boy and lover of misspelled names, had tapped her glass, and the guests fell silent, expecting a toast about how wonderful Nycholiss was.

"I have something to say," she began, her voice hard. "Yes, it's my son's birthday, and happy birthday, Nycholiss. But I think everyone here should know that Winnie Smith, my party planner, has been sleeping with my husband. Don't even think about denying it, Winnie, and shame on you for being the kind of woman who's willing to break up a family. You're disgusting."

All eyes swiveled to Winnie. Winnie herself glanced behind her, thinking for a flash that maybe Blakelee was talking about another Winnie Smith. Blakelee's face was bright red, and Winnie felt a flash of sympathy for her, making such a scene at her kid's party. "Um...maybe you need a drink of water," she suggested.

"Don't patronize me, you homewrecking whore!" Blakelee shouted. "How dare you?"

"I...okay, you must be thinking of someone else," she said, her voice calm and firm. "I have not slept with your husband." Winnie had never even met Mr. Johnson (who hopefully had a normal name). But seriously. Winnie, some kind of side chick? Please. She *was* seeing someone, but he certainly wasn't married or a father. They were pretty serious, so everything else aside, she wouldn't have time to steal a husband. Nevertheless, everyone was staring at her, the joyful shrieks of the kids in the bounce house a dissonant backdrop to the anger on Blakelee's face. "I'm not sleeping with anyone's husband, Blakelee. Can I get you a glass of water? You look a little flushed."

"Of course I'm flushed! How could you possibly sleep with the husband of a client? Your website says 'family events' but you think it's okay to seduce the father of three?" Blakelee screeched.

"Stop," Winnie said, her voice hard. "I haven't slept with anyone's husband. I would never do that."

"You stay away from my family before I get a restraining order!" Blakelee said.

"You're *paying* me to be here," Winnie had said. "And you're wrong. I—"

"Does *he* look familiar?" Blakelee said. She shoved her phone in Winnie's face, and the ground seemed to evaporate from under Winnie's feet.

It was Mitchell, Winnie's boyfriend of the past six months, the man she slept with three or four nights a week. The man she loved. In the photo, he stood on the beach, arms wrapped around Blakelee, the three kids hugging their legs.

Did Mitchell have a twin, maybe? People mistook Addie and Lark all the time. That must be it. "I...he's not..." The words died in her mouth.

Nycholiss's party was outside. Winnie hadn't even been in the Johnson house. She and Blakelee had met just once in person to discuss this party, and that meeting had taken place at her sister's bookstore. She hadn't needed to go in this morning for setting up—everything was outside, the food table, the bounce house, the bubble station. Well, she hadn't gone in *yet*. In just ten minutes or so, she'd go in for the cake, and later, during cleanup, she imagined.

Suddenly, she was very, very worried that if she did go inside and take a look around, there'd be a photo of Blakelee's husband. Who was, it was slowly dawning, also Winnie's boyfriend.

Then her phone buzzed, and in a daze, she slid it from her pocket. A text from Mitchell.

> I think we should stop seeing each other

> It's run its course.

No shit, Mitchell.

This could not be happening.

"You didn't Google him? You didn't show anyone his picture? No one said, 'Hey, that looks like Tanner Johnson?' I call bullshit."

Winnie didn't know Tanner Johnson. She knew Mitchell Preston. Her legs felt wobbly, her head seemed detached from her body, Winnie turned, tried to say something to Blakelee, who then tossed her wine in Winnie's face.

Turned out the Mitchell Preston of Hyannis, the chef Winnie had been seriously involved with, was actually Tanner Johnson of Eastham, legal name Tanner Mitchell Johnson. Preston was his mother's last name. He'd been married to Blakelee for seven years, was the father of three adorable children with weirdly spelled names, and used a professional name for whatever reason...and so women like Winnie could be tricked into thinking he was single.

He had *never* mentioned a family. When she'd asked him if he'd ever been married before, he'd said, "Never got that lucky." There was not a single photo of a wife or children at his condo in Hyannis. Not one in the kitchen where he worked as the acclaimed chef of Nuage Bleu, as expensive and pretentious as the name implied. Mitchell Preston didn't wear a wedding ring or even have an indentation on his finger where one might have been.

Obviously, Winnie had googled the hell out of him, like any normal person would. She'd checked with the assessor's office in Hyannis, which had listed the owner of his condo as M. Preston. She had done her due diligence. She had.

Last March, Winnie had been sitting in the bar of Nuage Blue, waiting for Lark to finish her shift in the ER and join her for dinner. Her sister was running late, so

Winnie was scrolling through Pinterest, looking at cake ideas, when the chef came out, set out a sampler plate in front of her and introduced himself. He was single, he was attractive, he was employed. The unicorn of Cape Cod, in other words.

Turned out the unicorn was actually an ass.

Men. Liars. Bastards. Et cetera. It did not change the fact that until Nycholiss Johnson turned five, Winnie had been crazy in love, finally understood the fuss around sex, relationships, soulmates.

Blakelee's rant had the effect she no doubt intended. While it had to be true that Mitchell—Tanner—was also being trolled somehow, too, twelve clients had canceled. Some had been polite—*don't think we'll need you after all*. A few had been rude. *You must've tried VERY HARD to not know who he was.* One had been kind. *Tanner is an asshole, but I'm sorry, Winnie, my kids play with Blakelee's all the time.* Yesterday at Wellfleet Marketplace, Winnie had said hello to Courtney James, who ignored her. Winnie had been Courtney's wedding planner three years before. Winnie had stood there, flushed and ashamed and angry with Tanner, with Courtney and mostly with herself. There had to have been a way for her to learn this before.

Like a lot of people in their thirties, Winnie had long ago grown weary of social media. She had an account for her business, but not a personal account, because most of her family and friends were local. If she wanted them to see a picture of the sunset, she'd text it. And she thought posting pictures of herself and Mitchell was kind of tacky. Bragging. *Look at me and my boyfriend! I have a partner! Do you???* Plus, she hadn't even been ready to share the news with her family, who had a tendency to swarm and assume and start making wedding plans and all that.

But if she had...damn it, if she *had* posted pictures on social media, someone would've instantly told her who Mitchell really was.

She'd Googled "Mitchell Preston, chef," and read all the articles. Not one had said the words *wife, married, children, kids.* Never. She'd stalked Mitchell Preston's social media sites (all food-related). Did one of those background checks to see if he'd been arrested or divorced, and no, Mitchell Preston, because he was a fake person, had not been. The M. Preston who owned his condo turned out to be Margot Preston, his mother.

She had done her best to vet him. Hadn't she? The Mommy Mafia didn't think so, and maybe she agreed with them. People saw what they wanted to see, after all.

But no. She had tried. Even so, the horror of being the other woman—and the shame of falling for a married man and father who had no problem lying for months—made her want to go down to the beach and howl into the wind.

"Let's do this," Rosie said, snapping Winnie's fuzzy head back to the moment. They went into the Ice House, the restaurant where trivia nights were held. "Head high, shoulders back, screw the haters."

"Right," Winnie said. One good thing about a big family —safety in numbers. Plus, no one would dare say anything about her when Grandpop was around.

They sat at the team's table, and Winnie said yes to another glass of wine. A few people looked their way, eyes gleaming with gossipy glee. Gleaming with gossipy glee. That was fun to think. A few hellos were called out to other Smiths, but no one said anything specifically to her.

So what? She didn't care. Well, of course she did, but she didn't, right? Gleeful gleaming gossips, that's what they were.

The game got underway, teams huddled at their tables, half the patrons just there to eat and drink and watch. As the DJ, Robbie's job was to read the questions and then play songs that sort of matched the answers. He did it well and with gusto. Everyone loved Robbie. Everyone loved Harlow and Lark. Grandpop practically had a statue in the center of town, he was so beloved. Lark was a minor celebrity just because she was so nice and sweet, *and* a doctor. Her parents, super popular, Dad a retired nurse, Mom the owner of a popular art gallery and gifted artist. Addie wasn't adored as much, but definitely envied and powerful.

Winnie...she had never made much of a mark. Until now. Until making the scarlet letter A. Oh, the irony! The irritating, ignominious irony! She laughed, tried to say those words to Grandpop, but saw he was deep in discussion about a trivia question she hadn't heard. She took another sip of wine. Or a slug. It was actually a slug.

Winnie didn't need to actually participate in the game because Harlow's team took this shit very seriously, pouncing like a great white on a wounded baby tuna. Anything science-based, Lark and Grady had down pat. Grandpop was the history buff, Rosie knew everything pop culture, Harlow nailed current events and literature. How many elements are in the periodic table? A hundred and eighteen, apparently. (Robbie played *She Blinded Me with Science* by Thomas Dolby). Who played Mrs. Robinson in the movie *The Graduate*? Anne Bancroft (Robbie blasting the Simon and Garfunkel song). Name Henry VIII's six wives. Katherine, Anne, Jane, Anne, Catherine, Katherine. (*Marry You* by Bruno Mars.) Robbie really was a good DJ.

Winnie listened and toasted Harlow and her teammates and drank more wine, as was her right. She even relaxed a little. The nachos were excellent. Did a person need more?

And then...then came the question that sank her leaky boat. "Which of these actors allegedly had an affair with his child's nanny?" Robbie read with gusto. "Your choices are A) Robin Williams, B) Ethan Hawke, C) Tom Hanks, or D) Arnold Schwarzenegger. Wow, that's a lot of cheating husbands, am I right?" Robbie said. He hit a button on his keyboard, then got up and headed to the bar with his empty water glass. From his speakers began the song.

The song that brought on her doom.

Jolene by Dolly Parton, in which a loving wife begs Jolene not to steal her man. And suddenly Winnie remembered that last week she was so in love that it felt she'd ingested pure sunshine. Mitchell had nuzzled her neck, murmured about how good she smelled, and she'd thought, *so this is love. It's all true.* Instead, she'd been a Jolene.

She jolted onto her feet. Where was Robbie? That song needed to stop immediately. He was chatting at the bar, blissfully unaware. "Robbie!" she shouted. "Robbie!"

He didn't hear her.

"I'm sure it's not intentional," Harlow said. "Robbie's just doing his job, Winnie."

"I love this song!" Grandpop said. "'Jolene, Jolene, Jolene, Jolene!'"

"Hey, Grandpop, maybe not right now," Dante said. "You know?" He gave Winnie a sympathetic look.

The penny dropped for Grandpop. "Oh, *dear.* I'm sorry, Winnie."

"No, it's fine," Winnie growled. But the song *was* a classic, unfortunately, and it seemed like a lot of people were following her grandfather's lead, begging Jolene not to take their man. Quite a few were looking at her. Some were now clapping their hands in time. How did so many people know the words, damn it? Oh. Robbie's projector had lyrics, like a karaoke machine.

The song finally registered for her idiot brother, and he leaped for his table. Not fast enough. Winnie stomped toward him and grabbed his mic. "For God's sake, Robbie! A little solidarity, maybe?"

"Sorry," he muttered. Laughter rippled through the restaurant.

"As for the rest of you," Winnie said, turning to face the restaurant patrons.

"Winnie? Winnie! Come sit with us," Lark said, standing.

"Winnie? Hon? Your food's here!" Harlow tried, waving a burger at her like Winnie was a dog (a trick which might have worked another night, to be fair).

"No," Winnie said. In the corner, Beth, owner of the Ice House, was waving her hand across her throat. Cut. Cut. Abort mission. Abort.

It was time to be heard. "You people," she began, dimly aware that beginning a speech with *you people* never ended well. "You people need to hear this. I didn't *know* he was married. Okay? I didn't. And for two, I'm pretty sure I'm not the *only* person in this room who's slept with someone else's spouse, am I? Not gonna name names, but I'm there in your houses, at your parties, and I see you eyeing each other. Maybe I see you sneaking into another room with someone who's not your partner at your stupid gender reveal parties and bridal showers and baby's first birthday party. Oh, yes, I do."

"Time for another question," Robbie called, raising his voice since he was now mic-less. "Where is the aqueduct of Sylvius? A) Rome, B) Peru, C—"

"It's in the human brain," Winnie said, though how she

knew that, she could not say. "And shut up, Robbie, I'm not done." No. Windsor Eleanora Smith was not finished. Nuh-uh. Nope. That fourth glass of wine had her back. "Let's talk about those parties, since we're all here. Can you all stop being so obsessed with your own lives? Do you *really* think your baby's gender needs a party to announce it? Can't you just pick up the phone and say, 'Hey, Mom, we're having a girl!' Can't you? Do you think the world needs to watch you pop your stupid balloons rain down stupid pink powder? Or how about your kid's first birthday? I've got news for you. All you're doing is overwhelming your kid. What *baby* needs fifty guests?"

There was silence, which she took to be encouraging. "And Jesus, the weddings!" she went on. "There is nothing more I hate than your weddings. Do you think you're the first person ever to get married!" She jacked up her voice to a jus. "'It's *my* day! I've been dreaming about this since I was in my mother's uterus! What should our hashtag be?' God! It's nauseating. Call me when you've *been* married a couple of decades and can still stand to look at each other, and *then* we'll have a party, because *then* you have something to celebrate other than the fact that you're an attention whore and—"

Her words stopped as Dante pried the mic out of her hand and practically lifted her away from the center of the restaurant.

"I'm not done," Winnie protested.

"Oh, you are," Dante said.

"Okay, then!" Robbie said.

"It was everyone except Tom Hanks," Rosie called. "Tom Hanks didn't sleep with the nanny."

Well, thank God for that. At least something was pure in this shitty world.

"Turning now to, uh, sports," Robbie said, microphone back where it belonged, "which of the following players won a Heisman Trophy? Was it A) our own St. Brady of Boston? B) Golden Joe Montana, C) Walter 'Sweetness' Peyton, or D) Devonta Smith, who my mother finds very attractive?"

Winnie was not sober, she recognized as her brother-in-law dragged her out of the bar and through the main dining room. Grandpop led the rest of them, saying things like, "Our dear Winnie is not at her best. Being accused of adultery has hit her quite hard," which was not helping.

"By the way, it was Devonta Smith," Dante said. "But everyone will say Tom Brady."

"What's wrong with you people?" Winnie said as he set her down on the sidewalk. "My heart is *broken*, and you're still answering trivia questions!"

Crying. She was crying. Harlow wrapped her in her arms and hugged her tight.

"I feel so stupid," she hiccupped.

"I know, honey, I know. We've all made huge mistakes when it comes to other people. It will get better."

Lark patted her shoulder, sympathy tears streaming down her face, and Rosie joined the hug as Winnie sobbed.

God. She hated crying. She hated *this*.

The air was damp and salty, the half-moon rising. No one spoke again. Winnie took a breath, then another. She wiped her eyes with the palms of her hands.

If her career hadn't already been over, it sure was now.

TWO

LORENZO

Lorenzo Michelangelo Santini—M.D., Ph.D., Chief of Special Surgeries at Mass General Brigham, Distinguished Professor at Harvard University Medical School, Fellow of the American College of Surgeons, winner of the Jacobson Innovation Award in Surgical Techniques, Member of the National Academy of Medicine, all-around God with a scalpel, known to terrified residents at four hospitals as Dr. Satan—was irked.

He'd just received an email informing him that the hotel where he was supposed to stay after delivering a lecture at the Mayo Clinic had water damage, and he would have to find other accommodations. His interview with *The New England Journal of Medicine* had to be rescheduled (or canceled, since the reporter clearly had no respect for his time). A book he had ordered should have arrived and had not.

He did not have time for these menial tasks. He was a world-renowned surgeon, for the love of God, and there were people for doing these kinds of lesser, time-sucking tasks. He just hadn't been able to find one.

In April, his sister, Sofia, had suggested he hire a personal assistant to help him manage his two homes (Chatham and Boston), someone who could schedule necessary workers like mechanics and landscapers, make his travel arrangements (that idiot from the Chicago conference had booked him in economy plus, not first class). This personal assistant would also pick up his dry cleaning, stock his fridge...all those tedious tasks people like Lorenzo shouldn't have to do. He wasn't being condescending. He was being honest. Was he *really* supposed to go to Whole Foods to buy kale when he could be, oh, saving a life? Teaching future doctors? Writing a paper that would change the way a procedure would be done, therefore raising patient survival rates?

An assistant made sense. He'd always had people to do things for him, of course—a travel agent, a cleaning service, the landscaper. But competence was hard to come by, and Lorenzo hated incompetence. Was it really so hard to tell the difference between fresh and dried basil? Skim milk and two percent? Did the travel agent really have to send seven confirmation emails, all of which Lorenzo had to read to be sure there was nothing relevant in them? He didn't want to wait on hold to get an appointment for his car to be serviced. Didn't want to have to call the florist himself to order flowers for his mother's birthday. It was enough that he even remembered his mother's birthday. Most years, he even called. He loved his mother, but you didn't get that time back, and it added up.

Sofia had recommended her friend Tillie. Foolishly, Lorenzo had hired her based on his sister's word alone. Tillie had lasted four hours. She had been "organizing" his kitchen (which was already perfectly organized) when he asked her to bring him an espresso. She had to be shown how to use the espresso maker. Then, twenty minutes after he'd demonstrated, she brought him a cappuccino instead. Lorenzo calmly told her that he did not drink cappuccino and she would have to try harder, listen better and be more intelligent than, say, a houseplant. Inexplicably, this made her burst into tears and quit.

He then called an employment agency on Cape Cod, where he tried to spend weekends and where his home needed more attention than his condo on Beacon Street. He was told he'd be placed on a waiting list, since demand for that kind of service was high. Lorenzo refused to be on any waiting list. A colleague at Mass General had recommended someone, and Lorenzo had contacted her and asked to set up an interview. She texted:

> Are you the one they call Dr. Satan?

When he answered in the affirmative, he never heard from her again.

After that, he contacted a high-end domestic employment agency—again, time that could've been spent on far more important things. They sent over three candidates. He didn't like any of them but hired one, then fired him a week later when he found the man sitting in his living room, reading.

"He was reading? My God, the nerve," Isabella, his younger sister, said when he reported this.

"Exactly. And sitting on the couch," Lorenzo said. Dante choked on a laugh, though Lorenzo wasn't sure why.

"You want Carson," Izzy said.

His younger sister was a nurse, though she could've been a doctor. Definitely smart enough. She'd gotten an A- in Organic Chemistry. He knew doctors who'd had to take that class *four times* before passing. Couldn't they see they simply didn't have the right stuff? Wasn't it obvious they were not meant to put their hands inside a human body? Many was the time when Lorenzo had informed a resident they were not cut out for medicine, not smart enough, not tough enough, not gifted enough. *Someone* had to say those things. Did the world want a C+ student from a fourth-rate college cutting into their child or spouse?

"Who is Carson?" he asked Isabella without missing a beat. His mind could hold on to dozens of facts at once and moved much faster than most people's. This was not bragging. It was simply a fact.

"A butler," Izzy said. "He never lets a detail slip, reveres the family he works for, and takes care of any and all problems without bothering his employer."

"Is he free?" Lorenzo asked.

"He's retired," Izzy said, and she and their mother laughed.

"Would Bates do?" asked their father.

"Dad, of course not. He's always in prison," Izzy said.

"You're not being helpful," Lorenzo said. Obviously, they were joking about something, though what, he didn't know. Popular culture, something he had no time for. He glanced to the head of the table, where his grandmother used to sit when she was alive, and felt a pang. *She* had understood him, at least.

"Anita, can I have some more eggplant?" asked Henry, Sofia's husband. The entire family was gathered for Sunday dinner, which, though held weekly, Lorenzo only attended every other month or so.

It was September now, all the students back in school. A busy time of year for him. He'd endured the traffic from Boston to attend this dinner. The house has been his gift to his parents when his dad retired, and it was large and beautiful, on the bay side of Falmouth, with a dining room that could seat twelve, a chef's kitchen—both parents loved cooking—and plenty of bedrooms for grandchildren, though they only had two at the moment. Sophia and Henry had just had Lucy, who was sleeping upstairs, and William, age almost three. The child stared at Lorenzo, eyes wide. Lorenzo raised an eyebrow, and William burst into tears. Henry scooped him up, then passed him to Lorenzo's mom, who made soothing sounds and kissed the boy's hair.

Lorenzo sighed. He probably should've spent this afternoon working. He always felt a little awkward with his family; he never got their inside jokes (who *were* Carson and Bates?) and often found it hard to talk with his siblings, who always seemed eager to poke fun at him.

"I might know someone," said Lark, his brother's wife. "How about my sister?"

"I didn't think your sister worked," Lorenzo said. Lark's twin was one of those vapid people who seemed to exist only to post on social media.

"My other sister."

"Did the bookstore go bankrupt, then?" Lorenzo asked. Not surprising. Independent bookstores were notoriously susceptible to failure.

"No," Lark said, her tone holding a note of irritation. "My other sister."

Ah. The rude one. "Have I met her?" he asked, though of course he had.

"Believe it or not, she was at our wedding, Lorenzo," Dante said. "Winnie. The youngest sister."

"And you met at Joy's house, before we, uh, broke up," Lark said.

Yes. They'd had a brief and terse exchange then. He

remembered the flash of irritation he'd felt. In the lead-up to Sofia and Henry's wedding, Lorenzo had asked Lark to be his companion. It had been a convenient arrangement, nothing more, meant to reassure his grandmother, then ninety-nine years old and failing, that he wouldn't end up alone. Not that there was anything wrong with that. Ninety-six percent of the time, solitude was quite appealing. At any rate, while he and Lark were pretending to date, she had struck up a friendship with Dante, and after Sofia's wedding, they started dating and got married. It had all been absolutely fine with him.

"Is this sister looking for work?" Lorenzo asked.

"She's between jobs at the moment." Lark said, exchanging a look with Dante. "She's organized and straightforward," she added. "I think you'd get along."

"She'd be a good fit, brother," Dante said. "She'd stay out of your way and get things done."

"I might need her on site in Chatham and Boston," he said. "And I'd have to be able to fire her without you bursting into hysterics, Lark. No offense, but you do cry disturbingly often."

"Tears of joy since she met me," Dante said, and everyone else laughed.

"No offense taken," Lark said, "and I understand. Never hire someone you can't fire."

"Exactly." He gave his sister-in-law a nod of appreciation. "All right. Give me her contact information. And thank you," he added. He wasn't a boor, after all.

"Good job remembering your manners," Dante said, and Izzy snorted, and Sofia looked at her plate, smiling. Lorenzo didn't know what was funny.

"Have some more chicken, Lorenzo," his mother said. "You love my spezzatino."

It was true, he did, and he had a ten-mile run scheduled for later to make up for all this starch. The protein would be useful. "Thanks, Mom," he said.

"You're a good son," she told him. "And brother."

He was. He knew that. Hadn't he bought his parents this very house? He'd paid for Sofia's dream wedding, paid off college for Isabella and started college funds for Lucy and William. He'd even offered to help Dante buy a home, though his brother had turned him down.

And yet the family humor flowed around him, making him feel a little left out, a little bit like a small boy looking out the back window of a car at his family as he was driven away.

TWO DAYS LATER, Winnie (an odd name) sat in Lorenzo's living room in his Boston apartment as he read her resume. Event planning business, seven years, four as business owner. That would involve a solid set of organizational skills, he assumed. She had included some online customer reviews, all five stars. *Winnie was lovely to work with.* He didn't care about loveliness. *Extremely organized.* That was more like it. He scanned the reviews and found the word *efficient* six times. Before that, office manager for an obstetrical practice in Wellfleet. Excellent references attached from both the midwife and doctor.

"How old are you?" he asked.

"Isn't it illegal to ask that?" she answered.

It was. But if Lark was her older sister, then this one must be in her early thirties, he guessed. She looked older. Not as pretty as Lark. Rather plain. Hair in a tidy bun (professional, which he appreciated), an unremarkable navy suit, and sensible, plain shoes good for walking the cobbled streets and uneven sidewalks of Boston. Practical.

"I have a heavy travel schedule for the next few months," he said. "I'm teaching, speaking and advising for five organizations. The ACS, the ASA, the NIH, Médecins Sans Frontières, and The Royal Academy of Surgeons. I assume you know what those are?"

"I do."

"Demonstrate, please."

Did she just roll her eyes? "The American College of Surgeons, the American Surgical Association, the National Institutes of Health, Doctors Without Borders, and the British equivalent of the ACS."

"Correct." He was a little surprised, he admitted to himself.

"I'm aware that you're a surgeon. I did some research."

"Good. If you work for me, you *should* be aware of who I am and what I do. I have a stellar reputation as one of the top surgeons in the United States, if not the world, as demonstrated by the frequent requests for me to conduct seminars, teach and lecture around the country and internationally."

"Mm-hm." She didn't seem impressed.

He narrowed his eyes. "You'll need to organize my travel, accommodations—I have high standards for both—and make sure I have the amenities I need." The last time he'd gone to a conference, he'd forgotten his shaving kit and had been given a cheap disposable razor by the hotel. Nicked his chin. "On the domestic front, you'll have to manage subcontractors, arrange for repairs, make sure things are the way I like them." His last housekeeper had seemed unable to fold towels in thirds, which made them untidy in the closet and therefore irritating. She also bought the wrong kind of cleaner, despite him giving her a list, and he'd had a headache from the fake lavender scent. He looked back up at her. "I may ask you to maintain my calendar and handle professional correspondence. Is all that clear?"

"It is."

He liked that she didn't make unnecessary conversation. Nor did she seem intent on making him like her, which he also appreciated. If she was efficient and quiet and had an eye for detail, he didn't need to like her.

"You'll probably have to spend overnights here and in Chatham. There's a guest suite down the hall with its own bathroom, and the lower floor of the house in Chatham has three bedrooms and a family room you can use. Will that be a problem?"

"No."

"Where do you live now?"

"Wellfleet."

Again, the brevity was pleasing.

"As for our families being tied...that won't be an issue?"

"I can't see how. Your brother is married to my sister. Otherwise, I barely remember you."

Lorenzo looked up abruptly. That was *his* line. "I recall you being rude to my grandmother."

"Yes. But she was rude first."

"A ninety-nine-year-old woman was rude to you? I doubt it."

"I said it was nice to meet her, and she told me she didn't like my face. Or me. That's fairly rude, I'd say."

It did sound like Noni. He looked again at Winnie's papers. No red flags. "Why don't I hire you for a trial period? Three months, and if you last that long, we can renegotiate."

"Sounds good."

That was it? No talk of pay, or time off, or benefits? "Do you have any questions?"

"I don't. Do you?"

Why would he? "No. I'll email you a list of your duties and my schedule. For now, you'll start in Chatham, so plan on being there tomorrow by 8:30 a.m."

"Will do. Thank you," she said. She offered her hand, and he was pleased that she had a firm grip. Then she was gone, as matter-of-fact as he could have asked for.

Still...she barely remembered him? That wasn't something he heard often. Ever, now that he thought of it.

Well. He'd make a list of things he wanted her to handle, and just the thought of not having to buy kale or call a hotel for an upgrade made his shoulders drop a centimeter or two.

THREE

WINNIE

Somebody thinks very highly of himself, doesn't he? Winnie thought as she drove back to the Cape after the interview. Plus, could they not have done this on Zoom? Instead, she'd had to drive two hours there and three hours back, thanks to the traffic at the Cape Cod Canal. When Lark started fake-dating him, she said that his nickname was Dr. Satan. Dr. Dull was more like it.

This was Winnie's third encounter with Lorenzo Santini. He had not improved with time.

The first time was when Lark was fake-dating him because he wanted his rude and ancient grandmother to think he was with someone before she died. Which would've been sweet...if Lark hadn't been a doctor down on her luck and Lorenzo someone who could influence her career. Sounded like a power imbalance to Winnie, and she'd said so. But Lark hadn't actually minded—said it had been kind of fun, really. But Lark was a lot nicer than Winnie.

The second time they'd met him was at Lark and Dante's wedding, which Winnie had helped plan. Lorenzo had been best man, and Winnie had asked him if he needed anything. He'd said no. His speech had been adequate. Otherwise, they hadn't interacted.

Today, the third time, cemented her impression that Lorenzo was arrogant, condescending, and as charismatic as a box of old dirt. Yes, yes, he was a brilliant surgeon, but Winnie didn't need surgery, so she was free to dislike him.

But she did need a job.

When she got back to the little house she was renting from her cousin, she tossed her bag on the counter, changed out of her suit and into shorts and a T-shirt. It was mid-September, the bulk of the tourists gone, the days still warm. She was starving, having ignored the siren song and salty scent of Burger King in Hyannis, The Knack in Orleans, Mac's Seafood in Eastham and PJ's in Wellfleet. She was on a tight budget. She also hadn't been grocery shopping since Fallyn Doane had called her a slut in Stop & Shop last week. For one, slut-shaming was so Boomer. For two, did any of Blakelee's friends have normal names? (Then again, she was named Windsor, since her mother had been obsessed with Queen Elizabeth.) There in the dairy section, Winnie had stopped cold, turned and stared at Fallyn until the other woman wheeled her cart in the other direction.

But still. It wasn't fun.

Her cupboards showed cereal and peanut butter. The fridge held a nearly empty bottle of white wine and a stick of butter. A reflection of her soul these days, this empty kitchen. Until two years ago, she'd lived with her parents— not a life goal, but such were the real estate facts of today. The Cape was an expensive market, and rentals were sky-high because of the tourist season. But then Cynthia, their cranky, sixty-something cousin, had gotten married. Winnie asked if she could rent the place from her, and Cynthia, less cranky thanks to her husband, said yes. The house was small and plain—a square, unimaginative cinder-block house, no basement, tiny yard, unrenovated since its construction in the fifties. But it was across the street from Mayo Beach, and Winnie could sit on the lawn chair and stare out into Massachusetts Bay in the crook of the arm-shaped Cape.

If she could afford it, Winnie would buy it, but Cynthia's little place, once considered a step above a shed, would now be worth close to a million dollars. Maybe more.

Until it had imploded, Simple Celebrations, her event planning business, had been doing well. Not as profitable as it had been when it had been owned by her former boss, Hannah Chapman, who had focused on very high-end weddings. But Winnie had wanted something more down to earth, more homespun, and less luxurious. Events geared to the year-rounders, not the bazillionaires who came to their huge houses for a month a year, or the brides and grooms who came here for their seven-figure weddings. Her business plan was to do more events on lower budgets. It had filled a niche in the market, and Winnie had hit the ground running—a good word from Hannah before she moved to France, the solid Smith family name and her own steady hand, determination and strong work ethic.

And then came Mitchell. Or rather, Tanner.

Winnie was not a romantic at heart. She bore witness to her parents' enduring love story, saw the solid marriage of Addison and Nicole, was thrilled that Harlow had married the nicest guy in town. She had watched Lark fall for Lorenzo's much more charming brother, then marveled when Robbie and Rosie got engaged.

All that being said, she held no hopes for herself. She

wasn't the type. She was too practical, too steady, too smart to believe that romance would hit her. She had never swooned. Never really even felt lust, to be honest. Online dating, while still the best way to find a partner, felt about as fun as prison, and the stories she heard were sometimes hilariously awful, sometimes downright scary. So she'd pass. She understood that some people wanted all the feels, the drama and romance. She had never been one of them.

Until Mitchell had placed the appetizers down and smiled at her. They chatted, Winnie not giving out too many details, being addicted to *Dateline* in both podcast and television forms. When Chef Mitchell Preston returned to the kitchen, she was more interested in his food than in him.

Two minutes later, he was back. "I know I just met you," he said, "but would you possibly want to, uh...um... meet sometime? You...I..." He blushed. He *blushed*. "I'd like to get to know you a little more. I...well. This is stupid, but I feel...Jesus, Mitchell, stop talking." He rolled his eyes at himself, shook his head and said, "Would you like to go out sometime?"

Windsor Smith did not have that effect on men. Ever, and yet this guy was babbling around her. Huh.

"Sure," she said, more curious than anything. She pulled out her phone, asked for his number, and then sent him a text.

Hi from Winnie.

His face lit up like the sunrise.

Weird. But there was a gooey, warm feeling in her stomach as he beamed at her and backed through the swinging kitchen doors. The bartender gave her a look, raised his eyebrows, and said nothing.

Later, Winnie would realize that was Mitchell's M.O. She'd realize the bartender's look and silence meant *so you're the next one* and also, *he's my boss so I can't say anything* and maybe *you're an idiot if you fall for this.*

She had fallen. Hard.

He thought she was funny, one of the few to catch her dry sense of humor. Loved hearing about her family. Looked at her like she was beautiful, even though she wasn't. Lark and Addison were beautiful, Harlow nearly as gorgeous as they were. Robbie made women walk into signposts. But with Mitchell's deep brown eyes gazing at hers, his expression slightly dumbstruck, she suddenly wondered if maybe she was beautiful, too. His smile made it feel like she'd been living in a cold, wet country and he'd just dropped her off in the Caribbean. The first time they kissed, so much *feeling* had washed over Winnie she almost swooned, her legs weak, head swimming. Her. Winnie Smith, the boring one. She'd had sex before—a guy at Cape Cod Community College, where she'd taken a few classes. That had only happened because he was nice enough, and she figured it was time to get the virginity stuff over with.

But my God, sex with Mitchell...who was making those squeaking noises? Who was wrapping her limbs around a man, desperate to get a little closer? Who was kissing like she was about to die and he was the cure? Winnie Smith, that's who. With Mitchell, she was as bright and delightful as a daffodil. She was sexy and sensuous, moaning as he fed her a bite of food, shivering if he touched her hair. She was someone she barely recognized, and she liked this version of herself.

Right until she hated herself. But for six months, she

had been utterly, completely, desperately in love. And look where that got her.

The night after her Ice House speech, just to ascertain that she really had blown up her business, Winnie had asked Addie to show her the texts about her, since Addie knew every mother on the Outer Cape.

"You don't want to see that, hon," Addie said.

"Show me."

Wincing, Addie handed over her phone. The Mommy Mafia had been unsparing.

Okay, Tanner has never kept it in his pants, but are we really supposed to think she had zero idea he was married? Also, and this is mean, but her??? The mousy little Smith sister?

She "didn't know." Yeah, right. Hello, the internet was invented for a reason. Plus Blakelee posts his picture like every 10 minutes. Or at least she did.

I just wonder if W has gone after anyone else. I mean, she has access to a LOT of families, know what I mean?

And then…

Did you hear about her tirade about how stupid we all are? Okay, then! Guess I'll hire someone who actually cares about my baby's gender reveal.

She was unhinged at the Ice House the other night! She needs a therapist. Also, hello? We were your bread and butter, Simple Celebrations. Sorry you hate us.

Her company's Google and Yelp reviews, once boasting a 4.9 rating, were down to 2.8. Phrases floated in front of Winnie's eyes, making her stomach cramp.

Do NOT hire this company.

Unethical. Slimy owner. Dishonest.

Makes fun of clients.

Not what she appears.

She'd handed Addie's phone back to her without comment, went into her nieces' bedroom, read them a story about a duck, then went home and Googled "countries that accept Americans for permanent residence." Unfortunately, she didn't have enough money to pick up and leave, not without having a useful job, like nurse or engineer.

Well. She had a new job now, and she was actually relieved that Lorenzo Santini appeared to be about as emotional as a coffee table. It would be a very welcome change. His homes were far enough away from the Mommy Mafia that she'd have some peace—the Outer Cape felt like a different world from the mid-Cape and Boston.

She'd been standing in front of the open fridge too long. With a sigh, she pulled out the bottle of white wine, got a glass and went out to the little cement patio outside the house.

Not what she appears.

The thing was, Winnie was exactly how she appeared. She accepted that she was a background person, the forgettable Smith sister, the boring one. But she'd made that work for her. A behind-the-scenes person was exactly what you'd want for an event planner. *Organized, clever, friendly but not fawning, cool under pressure, and someone who always delivered a great event beyond our expectations.* That's what her reviews used to say.

Meanwhile, Mitchell's restaurant didn't mention his sliminess, his lack of morals. No wonder he used a different name professionally.

Her phone dinged with a text from Rosie to her and Harlow.

> Want to hang out, my lovelies? Mocktail for
> me, real thing for you?

I'm pretty whipped. Interview in Boston. It
went well, but it's early bedtime for me.

A hundred percent honest, because Winnie never lied.

Harlow answered, and then Rosie typed something else.
She knew they were checking in on her, and she appreciated it.

Another text, this time from Lark. The Smith family
radar had been activated.

Thinking of you, honey! How did today go
with Lorenzo?

A nearly identical one from Addie, sweetie instead of
honey. She answered them both. One from Grandpop.

I JUST WANT YYYOU TO KNnoW THTAT
YOU ARE A FINE PERSON MY DEAR
&ADN WHO MADE THESE LETtERS SO
SMALL IS THERE A WAY TO MAKE THEM
BIGGER FOR MY OLD EYES

She answered them all with the facts. *Fine. Got the job.
Start tomorrow. I'll come over and fix that for you, Grandpop.* Mom called, and Winnie uttered the same words.

Of course, she was not fine.

Mitchell's apartment had been so sterile. She just
thought he was too busy to decorate. Then there was the
way he said all the right things, how he'd moved in slowly. It
was not a hookup, no sir. They'd dated—properly, with late-
night dinners, walks on the beach, bike rides on the rail trail
—for *two months* before she slept with him. She was practically a pilgrim by today's standards.

Apparently, he liked to work for it.

Or she'd just been an easy target, this mousy Smith sister.

Addie had reported he'd been in church with his family on Sunday. *He* was the one who should've been ashamed, and yet shame seeped from every molecule of her. She'd *slept with another woman's husband*, hadn't dug deep enough to see if he was lying, somehow thought that a single, good-looking, talented guy would go for her.

Stupid.

She sat on the little patio and stared at the water, drinking. She should get a dog, she thought. Someone who'd truly love her. A Lexus drove by, the passenger window rolled down. A female arm extended, middle finger raised. Winnie waved back, pretending not to care.

Her phone chimed. A text from a 508 number.

> You should be ashamed of yourself.
> Everyone hates you right now, Winnie. How
> could you try to brake up that sweet
> family?

Winnie typed back.

> You mean "break," idiot. Also, bite me.

Then she blocked the number and chugged the rest of her wine.

Lorenzo had said she'd have to stay some nights. She went inside, opened her laptop, and sent him an email.

To: Lorenzo.Santini.MD.PhD.FACS@gmail.com
(for the love of God, that was a long address).
From: Winnie.E.Smith@gmail.com

Re: Staying over

Lorenzo, if it's convenient and you are in Boston, I would like to spend a few nights in Chatham to get a feel for what your household needs and to familiarize myself with the property. Please let me know if that's agreeable.

Winnie

Less than a minute later, she had an answer.

It is.

Thank God. If she had to stay in Wellfleet another minute, she'd burst into tears.

FOUR

WINNIE

She drove down to Chatham early the next morning. Since she would not be seeing the boss, she wore jeans and a T-shirt with a picture of an oyster on it. A list had landed in her inbox at 1:04 a.m. this morning, outlining her duties.

Please see that the house is cleaned with the products in the broom closet. Do not use any other brands. Arrange cleaning schedule for at least 1x/week.

Please do the laundry if there is any, using the products in the laundry room, nothing else. Do not use any other brands.

Grocery shopping, as I will be home this weekend. Items are below.

Check to ensure that I am not about to run out of staples by checking the pantry, cupboards and refrigerator.

Hire new landscaper asap. I saw weeds last weekend.

Schedule repair of stairs on deck. The wood is Brazilian ipe, sustainably sourced. No other wood will be considered.

Contact arborist for oak tree. One branch looks sickly.

Anything else you notice.

HIS FOOD NEEDS were a little stark... vegetables, fish, chicken breasts, mineral water, lemons, skim milk. Somewhat joyless, really. No ice cream, no chocolate, no ribeye.

She'd never been to his house before, but Chatham was probably the most expensive town on Cape Cod, and utterly gorgeous. Famed for its charming, crooked streets bursting with tidy, gray-shingled houses and lush gardens, as well as the great white sharks that swam offshore, Chatham had a bustling downtown, several gorgeous hotels and inns, and great restaurants.

She followed her GPS to Lorenzo's house, then pulled into the driveway, her mouth open in wonder. Lark had said it was beautiful. The word hadn't done it justice.

It was *stunning*. A huge green lawn with a few mature trees offered shade in the front, a curving slate walkway led to the front porch. The house was a mid-century modern, sleek, simple, and elegant with clean lines, an asymmetrical, angled roofline, and gray cedar siding. Winnie was something of a real estate hobbyist, checking the online sites once a day in case a unicorn home came on the market...something she could afford, in other words. Dr. Satan's home had to be worth millions.

The backyard led to a small set of stairs. Beyond that, the Atlantic, stretching all the way to Portugal. Wow. In something of a trance, she walked past the house—all those windows!—and down onto the beach. The waves were gentle, the tide going out, small lines and patterns rippling the sand with the breath of the ocean.

Suddenly, a large blond dog came running toward her, tail wagging, tongue lolling. "Hello, baby," Winnie said, reaching out a hand to see if it was friendly. She. The dog was a girl, a creamy golden retriever or close relative, and she was very friendly, sitting down and smiling at Winnie, her doggy eyes filled with adoration. "You are gorgeous." The Lark of dogs, so happy and giving and beautiful beyond compare. She petted the animal's silky head, checked for a collar, and found none. "I bet you live around here," Winnie said. "Do you? Do you have a nice house? Does your family know how lucky they are? Hmm?" The dog turned in a circle. Winnie picked up a stick, whitewashed by the ocean, and threw it, and the dog bounded away after it. Once she caught it, though, she continued down the beach, ostensibly toward home.

Sweet girl.

Well. Winnie had things to do. She walked around the house, the thick green grass as welcoming as a freshly made bed, though in need of cutting. A line of hydrangeas, their blossoms indigo, stood against one side of the house. Otherwise, not much in the way of a garden, flower or otherwise. She wondered what it looked like in the spring, if daffodils and tulips sprang up from the ground in a riot of color. Somehow, she doubted it. Dr. Santini seemed more like the color-coordinated type.

Imagine living here every day with that view, these sounds...the different voices of the waves and wind, the cries of seagulls and terns, the peeps of piping plovers in the evenings. It would be impossible to feel sad for very long, living here. She wondered if Lorenzo had bought this place to soothe his soul. He must face some pretty grueling days. Even Dr. Satan must lose a patient sometimes. She pictured him telling a family their loved one hadn't made it, putting a hand on their shoulders, telling him they did everything possible. Kind and strong, his voice low and somber, sympathy written all over his face...

Nah. He probably made an underling do it. A human, in other words. But he did get to live here, and for at least part of the time in the next three months, she got to spend time here, too. She'd make the most of it.

Inside, the house was just as beautiful as its setting. The front hallway was wide, the living room on one side, dining room on the other. Scandinavian or mid-century style furnishings, a little too spare for Winnie's taste, but all very tastefully done. A fireplace with an exposed, black-painted brick chimney. Pale gray walls. There was a huge painting she recognized as an Anne Packard, another from A. Paul Filiberto, both legendary Provincetown artists that any Cape Codder would recognize. A more modernistic (and uglier) painting hung in the dining room—slashes of yellow, white, black, and gray. She bet it cost thousands of dollars, though Imogen could probably do the same thing, more or less. The dining room table could seat eight comfortably.

The kitchen was a chef's dream—a six-burner gas range and double oven, Italian-made appliances, white quartz countertops, black cupboards, and gray, marbled tiles in a honeycomb pattern making up the backsplash. There was an island that could seat four, as well as a small round table with two chairs.

She wondered if she could bake here. Even in her current house, where the kitchen had about twelve inches in counter space, she baked at least twice a week, funneling the goodies to Grandpop and Robbie, the former because any kind of sweets delighted him, the latter since he had four older sisters and was thus helpless. Baking in this kitchen would be like having her own show on The Food Network.

At the end of the hall was the large owner's suite, looking about as personal and welcoming as a hotel. More gray walls, a darker gray comforter on the bed, four stark white pillows. Tasteful but dull. There was a single family photo on his long, low dresser—his family at his sister's wedding, the one Lark had gone to. Everyone was laughing except the tiny grandmother, who stared directly into the camera, and Lorenzo, who looked somber and handsome. She studied the photo, wishing he was smiling, too. Then again, it was just a photo. Surely, he'd smiled and laughed with the rest of them. Lark had said it had been one of the most beautiful weddings she'd ever been to.

There were two other bedrooms on this floor, each with en-suite bathrooms, also furnished with Scandinavian style, plain-but-handsome furniture. Chilly. Nothing that indicated he was a doctor, or had hobbies, or a penchant for, oh heck, dogs playing poker. Just a lot of blank walls and spectacular views.

Winnie spied a spiral staircase, went down it, and there was another story, this one at beach level. There was a more casual living room with a huge TV on one wall, a fireplace, empty bookcases and no other furniture. Hm. Guess he (or his interior decorator) hadn't gotten around to this area. The hallway led to two more bedrooms, smaller than those upstairs and more unfinished looking—no pictures on the walls, empty closets and bureaus. She chose the one that overlooked the water. It was painted the same pale gray as the rest of the house. The comforter was white, and there were no shams or throw pillows to warm it up.

She had mentioned the view, though, right? A sliding glass door opened directly into the backyard and sea beyond. Winnie opened the door and stood for a minute, listening to the song of the Cape—water, birds, wind. No human sounds, not at the moment. Yes. She could live here for a while and let her stupid heart heal.

Because if she let her guard down for just a minute, the truth of the word *heartache* twisted in her chest. It had been two weeks since Blakelee's party. Two weeks since she'd been in love with a man who did a helluva job making her think he loved her, too. And God, it had been *amazing*. The warmth in his eyes, the thrill of being part of a couple, the almost surreal happiness of lying in bed with him. He cooked breakfast for her every time she stayed over. (Four times. That should've told her something, all those nights when he told her, regret on his face, that he needed a good night's rest, and "I sure don't feel sleepy around you, Winnie.") But that was the thing! He'd made such incredible statements, things that a guy in love should not have been able to come up with. "It's hard to remember a time without you" and "I've been waiting all day to hear your voice."

Winnie wished she could tell Blakelee how sorry she was. She wished she could apologize to those cute little kids. *I didn't mean to take him away from you. He should've been home. He should've been with you. I didn't even know you existed. I'm so sorry.*

She could've looked harder. Should have, obviously.

Last week, while she was still wallowing in fury and hurt, she'd fallen back into the internet rabbit hole of stalking. There had been one article from seven years ago that she had read...mostly. It was from one of those lifestyle magazines, and she could only read six paragraphs before the paywall asked her to subscribe. She'd opted not to the first time, when she'd just met him. This time, she coughed up the four dollars. And had she done that six months ago, she would have seen the seventh paragraph—the one that said, *The chef, who formerly used his legal name Tanner*

Johnson at Bon Vivant in Boston, wanted a fresh start on Cape Cod.

There it was. She should've dug deeper back then, because she would have googled Tanner Johnson, Cape Cod, chef, and found out exactly who he was, and she would've blocked his number and not given him another thought.

The liar. The lying liar of Lie-Land had made her, the straightforward and unremarkable, unemotional and logical Smith child, a messy queen homewrecker baddie.

The remembered quiet of her single life—the time before Mitchell-Tanner—flooded back hard. For six months, her world had been filled with buzzes on her phone from his texts, his warm voice when he called her (so old-school). She hated that she missed the anticipation of having somewhere to go, someone to wait for. That weird, new happiness brought on by stopping by Nuage Bleu an hour before closing, sitting at the bar and catching glimpses of him, waiting for him to finish the night and take her back to his place.

She missed a man who didn't exist in real life. She missed the woman she'd been in that fiction.

"Knock it off, Windsor," she said to herself, her voice flat and stern. "Live and learn."

She unpacked her clothes—just shorts, shirts, jeans and a sweater, plus two bathing suits, because she wasn't going to let that beach go to waste. Then she got out her list, found the credit card Lorenzo had left for her in the kitchen, and drove into town to buy groceries.

FIVE

LORENZO

Winnie Smith's very plain electric car was in the driveway when Lorenzo pulled his Lamborghini next to it Thursday evening. He'd have to ask her to park in the garage, because a gray hatchback with a few dings and four shark-positive bumper stickers did not fit his home's aesthetic. He could've alerted her that he was coming home a day early and sent her home, but he wanted to surprise her in case she was sprawled on his couch, eating potato chips and scrolling through her phone. He could send her home after he assessed her work.

She didn't seem to be there, however.

"Ms. Smith?" he called. No answer. He supposed he should call her by her first name, ridiculous though it was. Who named their child after a fictional bear?

He opened the door. The house smelled...different. Pleasant. Lemony, perhaps, with a hint of yeast. It was immaculate. Well, it was *always* immaculate, but Lorenzo appreciated the *fresh* cleanliness. Often, the air felt stale, since the house could go unoccupied for two or three weeks. But today, the windows were open to let in the salty, fresh

September air. Also, she'd opened each window six inches exactly, he judged (and he was a surgeon, so he could guess distance to within a half millimeter). The symmetry was pleasing.

The maple end tables, bookcase, and coffee table gleamed in the golden light of the late afternoon. There was a vase of red dahlias on the dining room table (on a coaster, he was glad to note, because that table was an original Mies Van Der Rohe, and if she left a water stain, he'd have to fire her). Another vase sat in the middle of the kitchen island, the blood-red color pleasing against the black and white of the kitchen. On the counter was a glass bowl of lemons and, on the other side of the sink, a narrow wooden tray with four orangey-red tomatoes in a line, stems down, and a round loaf of bread under a cake dome.

It looked almost like someone lived here. Hm.

He opened the fridge and saw that it was stocked with the items he'd requested. The asparagus was sitting in a wide-mouthed mason jar, the ends in water, as appropriate. Same with a healthy bunch of parsley. Bottles of mineral water were lined up precisely. A dozen brown eggs sat piled gently in a green ceramic bowl, more pleasing than seeing them in an egg carton. A glass bottle held what appeared to be skim milk. There was chicken, carrots, kale, radishes, plain yogurt, everything neatly arranged. Though he hadn't asked for it, there was also a glass pitcher of water with cucumber slices. He'd never had cucumbers in water. It might be refreshing. In the cheese drawer, there was a selection of cheeses, though he didn't often eat cheese.

The pantry was also stocked with his requested items. In addition, there was a bottle of Brennevin, the Icelandic liquor he enjoyed, though he didn't drink often. He frowned. He hadn't put that on the list, and it was not an obvious choice of alcohol. There were also three bars of Tony's Chocolonely 70% dark chocolate, the wrappers tawdry and bright.

"Hello," came her voice.

Lorenzo turned. Winnie Smith stood in his kitchen, her straight hair pulled back in a severe ponytail. Though she stood a good five feet away, he caught a hint of her soap—clean, sharp, and simple. It triggered a memory of his childhood. Ivory soap, that was it. Noni had kept bricks of it in the linen closet to discourage moths. When he'd first come to live with his grandmother, he'd hidden in that closet so she wouldn't see him cry. Not a pleasant memory, so he dismissed it and continued to look at his new assistant. Her face was devoid of makeup, and she wore a white shirt and jeans that stopped above her ankles. On her feet were sandals.

"Please don't wear shoes in the house," he said.

She bent down and slid off her shoes, then straightened, holding them in her hands. "I wasn't expecting you until tomorrow," she said.

"Yes. A surgery was canceled." Irritating, really...the patient had come down with a fever, and the surgery was a McKeown esophagogastrostomy, which Lorenzo always enjoyed, since he got to open the neck, chest *and* abdomen in one procedure. Plus, complications were common—a leak at the anastomosis or pulmonary issues. Lorenzo had yet to have a patient suffer any, which was always a point of pride.

"You have a long weekend, then," Winnie said. "Would you like me to go?"

"Don't you work for me now?" he asked. Surely there were things to be reported. He wasn't used to having a personal assistant. It seemed that she should, oh, have something to do here.

"Yes. But if you want to be alone, I can go—"

"How do you know I drink Brennevin?" he asked.

"—back to Wellfleet and work from home." She scowled as she talked through his interruption. "In answer to your question, I asked your brother what kind of things you liked, and he said Brennevin, so I got some. You had nothing fun to eat or drink on your list, so I thought I'd add a few things."

"Chocolate?"

"Dark chocolate. It's good for you."

The sun on her hair made it look reddish-gold, and her skin was lightly tanned, her cheeks looked freshly pink. He should warn her about sunscreen. Then again, she should already know. The whole world knew. "Dark chocolate is not good for you," he said.

"It lowers your blood pressure and helps with brain function." She folded her arms across her chest.

He scoffed. "So candy manufacturers would have you believe. Actual science has debunked that myth."

She blinked pointedly. "Okay," she said, her tone implying he was being irrational. "I'll pay you for them and eat them myself."

"Good." Actually, dark chocolate wasn't exactly *bad* for a person if you ate an ounce here or there. Maybe he'd keep one bar.

"I just emailed you a list of things I've done today," Winnie said. "Why don't you check it and see if there's anything else you need from me? If not, I'll head home."

Again, she was telling him when she could go. Irritating. "Why did you buy flowers?" he asked.

"Because they were pretty. I thought they would cheer the place up."

"The *place* doesn't need cheering up. It's an architectural gem."

She raised an eyebrow, but said, "It is. Even so, flowers make everything nicer. Again, if they bother you, I'll pay for them and take them home."

"And that bread? Where did that come from? I avoid processed foods."

"I made it."

That explained the yeasty smell in the air.

"Why did you buy cheese?"

"In case you had people over, since the weekend is almost here, and I know your family lives nearby. Maybe you have friends. This way, you could offer them something other than an asparagus stalk or a basil leaf." She paused. "I also bought a few bottles of wine in case you did have company."

He had no plans for company. Nevertheless, she had only started yesterday, and already his fridge was full, his house was clean, and his favorite alcohol sat waiting.

"Let me review your list," he said.

"Sure. Would you like something to drink?"

"Water, please. You're welcome to have some, too."

"Gosh, thanks," she said. She poured them each a glass from the pitcher. "Would you like a glass of whatever Brennevin is?"

He considered it. He did indeed have a long weekend. "Yes, please. Again, you're welcome to some as well." Drinking with employees was probably not a good idea, but A) she was his brother's sister-in-law, and B) it was 4:42 p.m. He supposed she was off the clock, though they hadn't discussed her hours or, for that matter, her pay. "What is your hourly rate, by the way?" he asked.

"Two hundred dollars an hour," she said.

"Fine. Bill me weekly, please."

She spun around. "Oh, I was joking, Lorenzo. That's too much."

"Is it?"

"Yeah. I'd guess the going rate is somewhere closer to fifty."

So he'd pay four times the going rate and hopefully get four times the quality and commitment. "Two hundred is fine."

"Um...okay, well, I guess you can be the judge of that." She poured them both glasses of cucumber water, then took a martini glass out of the freezer, then opened the Brennevin.

A chilled martini glass. Very 1950s. He approved. "If you make my life run more smoothly, it will be money well spent. Please, come sit in the living room while I look over your list."

"Let's go out on the deck. It's a gorgeous night."

He didn't like being directed in his own home, but she had a point. He took the water and the martini glass and followed her outside. The smell of the ocean and sunshine, the blue of the sky and the call of the birds reminded him why he bought this place. The cushions on the deck furniture were clean and plumped. More red dahlias in a vase. "I don't want that vase being knocked over by the wind," he said.

"I put rocks in the bottom to weight it down. Barring a nor'easter, it'll be fine."

He wasn't sure he wanted rocks in a rare McCoy emerald green vase, but at least she'd had the foresight to secure it. She sipped her water and smoothed back a strand of hair the wind had freed from her ponytail. Definitely some reddish hues in there.

Lorenzo sat down, took a sip of his drink and looked at his phone, calling up her email.

1. Contacted carpenter about deck stairs. He can start on Monday and is coming by tomorrow to measure for materials.
2. Restocked pantry and fridge (itemized bill attached).
3. Fresh sheets and towels in all upstairs bedrooms / bathrooms, since you said it's been about a month since you fired your housekeeper.
4. Picked up dry cleaning.
5. Cleaned house (dusted, vacuumed, washed floors, cleaned first-floor windows).
6. Reorganized linen closet.
7. Called three landscaping companies to come by for quotes. One will come tomorrow morning, the others on Monday. Made sure they all do weeding, pruning, spring and fall cleanup, and snowplowing in addition to lawn cutting.

"How did you fold the towels?" he asked.

"In thirds." She didn't seem to think it was an odd question.

"Two hundred dollars an hour it is," he said, putting away his phone.

"It really doesn't seem fair. Doctors make less than that."

He almost laughed. "*That's* not true."

"Ask my sister. It is true."

Well, Lark was only an emergency room physician, but even so. Lorenzo took another sip of Brennevin, the warmth of the alcohol a perfect balance to the cooling fall air.

"You seem very efficient," he said, looking at Winnie. "Why did you leave your last job? You had your own business. Being a personal assistant, even for someone at my level, seems like a step down."

She gave him an undeniably irritated look. "'Someone at your level?'"

What had he said that earned that look? "Yes. I don't have a self-esteem issue, that is true. Why did you close your company? Or did you sell it?"

"I closed it."

"Why?"

"Personal reasons. I still have some events to do. My brother's getting married, and I'm their wedding planner. I'm putting together an anniversary party in October for an older couple. But it's a small job. I'm barely even charging them. It won't get in the way of my work for you."

"Why aren't you charging them?"

"Because it's their sixty-fifth anniversary, and they're fifth-generation Cape Codders. He wants to surprise his wife, and based on their house and car, it didn't seem like he could afford much, so I told him my fee was a hundred dollars."

"And how much would it cost them if he was wealthier?" he asked.

"Maybe two grand."

"Sounds like a very weak business model, charging five percent of what your time is actually worth."

She looked at him, her face devoid of expression. "It's not about profit in this case. I wanted them to have a nice party, so I'm donating my services. It happens among us humans."

Ah, the old robot innuendo. Certainly not the first time someone had used it. "I also donate my services," he said, his tone chilly. "And my services cost hundreds of thousands of dollars, so please adjust your tone."

"Do you need anything else from me?" she asked. "Or can I go?"

He paused. "I thought you'd be staying here. Aren't contractors coming over tomorrow?"

"You can't handle that yourself?"

"Winnie, the entire point of your employment is so I don't *have* to handle those things myself. You can go back to Wellfleet if you want, but it'll be a forty-five-minute drive each way. What time are the contractors coming?"

She paused. "Eight-thirty and nine."

"And were you planning to stay here if I was still in Boston?"

"Yes."

"Then stay. You have your own quarters, don't you? Have you chosen a bedroom yet?" She'd slept here for the past two nights, according to her notes.

"The smaller one downstairs," she said. "Overlooking the beach."

"Well. Do what you want. It doesn't matter to me, as long as you're back here before the contractors come."

She got up, then sat back down. "Fine. I'll stay. My car is electric, so I have to pop into town and charge it, anyway."

"Your car is also rather ugly. Would you mind parking in the garage?"

She gave him that look again, irritated and falsely patient. "Sure. I'll leave you to your evening, then, and I'll come back around..." She glanced at her watch, an inexpensive, Luddite kind, with hands and no access to the internet. "Around seven. Text if you need me."

"I won't," he said. "Enjoy your evening."

SIX

WINNIE

She was *not* enjoying her evening.

She'd gone into town, plugged in Chief Brody, her beloved electric car, and killed some time walking down Main Street as it charged. She'd just been in town this morning, so she didn't need anything, though the smells of garlic and seafood were wicked hard to resist. But good food in a nice restaurant reminded her of Mitchell. Her steps slowed as she passed a restaurant. There, seated at a window, was a couple about her age, smiling, talking. The woman reached out to touch the back of the man's hand, and they laughed about something.

She'd been like that. It was as alien as picturing herself living on Mars.

Just a couple of weeks ago, she'd pictured asking Mitchell to come as her date to Robbie and Rosie's wedding. She'd gone solo to her three sisters' weddings, happily so. But in this case, she'd imagined telling her family that yes, she'd been seeing someone, maybe it was getting serious, then fending off the barrage of questions that would follow. He'd come to dinner at Addie and Nicole's to meet everyone a few weeks before the big day, and his warm brown eyes would meet hers across the table. He'd see her as special, even in that happy, unruly mob.

One night about two months ago, he'd made her a late dinner at his barren condo, and he'd dropped a kiss on her shoulder as he passed by on his way to the stove. So much feeling—warm, gooey, hot-chocolatey love—bubbled up in her chest, and she took a breath, then hesitated. *Do it, Winnie,* she told herself. *He's special. Don't be so wary all the time. Don't blow it.*

"I never believed all this really happened," she said.

"Believed all what happened, honey?" Mitchell asked.

Honey. Her blood slowed and thickened to that same substance, thick and golden and sweet.

"Love," she said, blushing. Yes. She, Windsor Eleanora Smith, had brought up the subject of love. Had implied that she loved Mitchell Prescott before he had implied he loved her.

"It's definitely happening with me," he said, and then clothes were basically flying through the air, and they were laughing, and one of them was lying and the other was an idiot.

How long would it take for these memories to stop mugging her? She gave herself a mental shake and kept walking, past the great smells, the little bookstore, the churchyard with the darkest blue hydrangeas she'd ever seen, then made her way back to Chief Brody, who was now sufficiently charged at 62%, more than enough to get her back to Wellfleet tomorrow.

When she returned to Lorenzo's, she pulled her completely acceptable-looking-if-not-adorable car into his garage, eyed the Lamborghini with disdain and then walked across the yard to the back entrance to her *quarters,* as

Lorenzo had called them. The nicest servants' quarters in history, probably. Lorenzo clearly didn't come down here to watch TV, since there was no place to sit. What a waste. It would be amazing to watch a Patriots game down here.

Her phone buzzed with a text. Robbie.

> Hey, winona, what r u doing? want company?

Her mouth tugged. Robbie liked to pretend he was as deep as a piece of paper, but she knew better. She remembered how he cried when their oldest sister went to college, how he'd confided his adolescent love for Rosie to her (and only her, a secret she'd kept until two years ago). He'd bonded so easily with Matthew, the son Harlow had put up for adoption, and his deep friendship and love for Grandpop were totally pure. Granted, they all worshipped Grandpop, but he and Robbie were a fixture. Who else asked their grandfather to be best man?

> I'm at work, but thanks.

> How's the job?

Great! she typed, then deleted it

> Pretty well. Busy. Nice place.

> Cool. See you this weekend, yeah?

> Yeah. Rosie & I are talking flowers. Any favorites?

> Roses, obvs. 

Ew. You're so smarmy now. I kind of hate this side of you.

He sent a GIF of Betty White giving the middle finger. She couldn't top that, so she hit the laugh response and opened her laptop. She had a spreadsheet for their wedding, as she'd had for every event, from speed dating to funerals (yes, it was a thing). Robbie and Rosie's wedding would be Christmas-themed, all deep red, white and green, held at the gorgeous Chatham Bars Inn, which knew how to do luxe events.

Winnie didn't mind posh weddings when the bride was as casual as Rosie was (and when she was a guest who got to eat all that good food). After all, the money went to the local economy—the hotels, servers, florists, caterers, bridal shops, hair and makeup artists. Rosie was an easy client, loving pretty much everything Winnie showed her. Winnie had designed the invitation, two Rs facing each other, intertwined, roses spilling down the signs, and Rosie got tears in her eyes. "It's beautiful, Winnie. So special. I wonder what you'll do when your own wedding rolls around."

"Elope," she said. In that moment, she pictured her and Mitchell in a cute town in New Hampshire or Vermont.

Shit.

She tossed her laptop aside on the bed and went up the spiral staircase. She was starving, and the Tony Chocolonely bars were calling her name. Lorenzo stood at the complicated stove, a piece of fish in the frying pan, asparagus boiling in a pot next to it.

"You don't have a couch downstairs," she said. "It makes watching television a bit less comfortable."

He glanced at her. "I haven't gotten around to furnishing the whole house. And I don't watch television."

"Ever?"

"Very rarely. Order one."

"One what?"

"A couch. Something tasteful, please, in keeping with the aesthetic of the house. You can check the labels in the living room. Do *not* buy from a big-box store. Feel free to use the space while you work here. In your off-time, of course."

Gosh, she could sit on it and everything? "Okay."

She looked at the sad pot of boiling asparagus. "You know, asparagus tastes great if you grill it." He didn't comment. "Or at least steam it. You could put some butter in there if you want to actually enjoy it. Maybe some dill on the fish. And salt and pepper."

"Are you a chef?"

She was not, but Mitchell had, at the very least, given her some cooking tips. "No."

"Then save your input. I know how to cook a healthy dinner." He paused. "Do you want to join me?"

And eat that sadness right there? "Um..." She didn't have anything better to do, and she wasn't sure he'd allow DoorDash to come up his precious driveway, as they had last night with her order of fried dumplings and chicken with broccoli (also a healthy dinner, in her mind). "Will you put butter on mine, at least?"

"If you want to clog your arteries, then yes." He opened the fridge, got another filet and added it to the pan.

Was that an almost smile? More likely a mouth spasm from the thought of butter. She set the table in the kitchen, since she'd gone through his cabinets yesterday so she'd know where everything went (and because it was fun, seeing what he'd bought, what he still could use, getting the feel of this very elegant house). She took out cloth napkins, since he didn't have the paper variety, and set the table.

He brought their plates to the small kitchen table. Hers had two pats of butter melting on both the fish and the asparagus. No rice or couscous or potatoes, though. That was okay. She had peanut butter crackers in her car for emergencies.

She waited till he sat and put his napkin on his lap, then took a bite. "Not bad," she said. He didn't respond, but began eating himself.

Time to get to know her employer a little better. "Did you always want to be a doctor?" she asked.

"I always wanted to be a *surgeon*," he said, the implication clear. Plain old *doctor* would not have been enough, and given his personality, she really couldn't see him reassuring a mother of a young child or talking to a Gen-Xer about omega threes.

"And you like it?" she asked. "Being a surgeon?"

He gave her a puzzled look. "Of course. Why would I do it otherwise?"

"To help people, I guess. Heal the sick."

"Yes, that too."

"Lark mentioned they call you Dr. Satan at the hospital. My dad remembered that, too."

"Your father is a doctor?"

"A nurse. Well, he's retired now. Anyway, I gather you're hated and feared. Wicked cool nickname."

She could've sworn that one *was* an almost-smile.

"Did you like being an...event planner?" He grimaced slightly, letting her know what he thought of her field. She let it pass.

"Theoretically, yes. I got to be a part of the most signifi-cant moments of people's lives. Or at least, some significant moments." She paused. As she had said at trivia night, she thought some of the "events" were more narcissistic cries for attention / opportunities for Instagram posts. "When someone is celebrating something real, it's...rewarding to be involved with it." She paused. "You did that with your sister's wedding, right?"

"I funded it," Lorenzo said. "I told Sofia to do whatever she wanted and not think about the cost. My parents would never have been able to do that." He paused. "She was one of those women who'd been dreaming about her wedding since she was a little girl." He shrugged.

So condescending and smug...yet so nice, too, if he could tweak his words. She looked at him as he methodically cut up his asparagus spears. He was very good looking, she observed. Not her type, but his face was symmetrical, his eyes blue, his hair short and blond. Gorgeous cheekbones. But removed, somehow. His near-misses with smiling added some appeal. Then again, she didn't smile much either. Only when warranted.

Outside, the ocean sounded louder. Tide was coming in, and the moon was nearly full.

"How many Santini kids are there again?" she asked.

"Four. I'm the oldest, then Sofia, Dante and Isabella."

"I'm the fourth of five," she said. "I would've loved to have been the oldest." No comment. "Are you guys close?" she asked.

"Somewhat. I lived away from them when we were growing up. I went to a school for intellectually advanced boys."

"Oh." Her fish was gone. Plain but tasty. The same could not be said for the sad asparagus, however. She'd definitely be hitting some peanut butter crackers, *and* the rejected Tony's Chocolonely. "That must've been hard, being apart from the rest of them."

"Yes." He took a bite, chewed, swallowed, wiped his mouth, and then put down his fork. Clearly, a man comfortable with pauses. "But I lived with my grandmother and visited home when I could."

That sounded *very* hard to her. "You and she were close?"

"Very." His plate was clean, too. She bet he was still hungry, too. Too bad there was no dessert in sight. The bread she'd made had been hidden (or tossed).

"Let me clean up," she offered.

"Nonsense. You were my guest. Go order the couch and enjoy your evening."

Dismissed, albeit politely. "Okay. Thank you." She stopped at the pantry. "You sure you don't want this for dessert?" she asked, holding up the Tony's chocolate bar.

"I don't eat dessert."

"Ever?"

He sighed, clearly done with her. "I can't remember the last time I ate dessert."

"At Lark and Dante's wedding?"

"I passed."

His loss. Lark and Dante's wedding cake had been chocolate, and incredible at that. "Okay. Have a nice night, Lorenzo."

It was weird, being in the same house as someone she barely knew. Someone who didn't want to talk too much, who didn't watch TV. She listened for movement up above as she sat on her bed, scrolling on her laptop for couches that would match his austere style. She heard the slider open, then his footsteps on the deck. Good. The view was the best part of his "architectural gem." Because no matter how talented an architect or designer or landscaper was, no one could compete with the ocean. She put her laptop away, picked up her book (a dark historical fiction novel about World War II with absolutely no romance in it) and settled back against the pillows.

She fell asleep to the sound of the waves, and for the first time in weeks, didn't wake up until morning.

SEVEN

LORENZO

He should have had Winnie Smith come to the conference with him.

For the past several weeks, Winnie had quietly and efficiently done what he'd asked, and a bit more. Both his homes were running efficiently; she had vetted and hired housecleaning, landscaping, and dry-cleaning services. All of his bills were now paid automatically online. She had presented him with three options for new homeowner's insurance, scheduled payments for his property taxes and attended a meeting on his behalf with the ridiculous condominium association board for his place in Boston, effectively advocating for renovating the rooftop garden, as he'd instructed. She now ran his personal calendar, finding windows for him to run, attend the gym, call his mother. She even bought a slew of birthday cards for him to send to his family members. She drafted responses to the emails from grateful patients and family members, sent him lists of speaking and social engagements, and responded politely on his behalf. *Winnie Smith, Personal Assistant to Lorenzo Santini, M.D., Ph.D., Chief of Special*

Surgeries, Massachusetts General Brigham Hospital, Moseley Professor of Surgery, Harvard University Medical School.

He had to admit, he liked seeing her title. It made him feel...not safe, exactly, but protected. He had a gatekeeper, and she freed him from time-consuming, sometimes irritating tasks.

It wasn't awful to have her around, working in his office in Boston or at the house in Chatham. When he came home, she would give him a quick update on anything he needed to know, then disappear to her room. Sometimes, he thought, it might be nice if she had suggested they sit together on the deck, but he wasn't sure how to say this, and just left it alone. One day, he saw her down on the beach at his place in Chatham, throwing a stick to a big, blond dog, and he thought about joining her. He liked dogs. It looked like they were having fun. Just as he'd started down the deck stairs, though, the dog had run down the beach, and Winnie turned to come back in.

Whatever. She was a very good assistant so far, and he wished very much she'd been working for him when this particular trip to Chicago had been arranged. Alas, she had not been, and every single travel irritation had occurred— the car service had been late, making him rush through the airport, only to find his flight had been canceled. The next flight to Chicago was at midnight, and he'd had to fold himself into a seat in row 35. Then his luggage, which he'd been forced to gate-check, was somehow lost. He filled out a claim at the counter, jaw clenched, then finally left O'Hare.

When he checked into the hotel, he found himself in an ordinary room—not the suite he'd ordered and always chose. He went back to the desk, told them of the mistake, and was shown that, no, indeed, he had mistakenly booked the River

Room, not the River Suite. Full house, so no, he couldn't upgrade.

Without his luggage, he had to go shopping on Magnificent Mile (what a pompous name) and bought a new suit at Paul Stewart's, the sleeves of which were an inch too short. Nothing to be done about it, since he didn't have the time to get it tailored. He bought a shirt, a tie, and even socks and underwear. Then, when he'd gone back to the hotel, showered, dressed in the new clothes and was just about to go down to the conference, the desk attendant told him his suitcase had arrived.

Now, he stood in the area outside the conference rooms, his fellow doctors milling about and talking. Not his favorite thing, conferences. Too much glad-handing, too much small talk. He nodded to a colleague, scanned the room for someone who wouldn't be painful to talk to. He wasn't an introvert—he didn't think so, anyway. He just had other things he'd rather be doing. Surgery, for example.

There was Damian Hughes. Inwardly, he groaned.

Damian Hughes (pronounced Dahmmy-*ahnn*, something the man enjoyed correcting and repeating ad nauseam) was several years younger than Lorenzo. He had a solid CV—Notre Dame undergrad, Stanford Medical School, a fellowship in endocrine surgery at UCLA. But he was the type of doctor Lorenzo liked least—spending a lot of time announcing that he was the next savant in the world of difficult surgeries. He was not. Not yet, anyway. Rumor had it he had a TikTok channel and did something called reels on other social media platforms, which Lorenzo found juvenile and undignified. He himself did not have social media accounts, prescient enough decades ago to realize there would be no benefit to him to spew personal information out into the world.

It seemed Damian had a personal assistant with him. While many surgeons may have had such a staffer, it wasn't common to travel with him. A lover, perhaps? No, the man definitely gave off the impression of employee. He obsequiously brought Damian a bottle of water, head slightly bowed, handed him an iPad, and whispered something in his ear, all actions meant to telegraph Damian's status.

Damian wore a pale lavender suit and somehow made it look...good. The man always dressed as if he were Ryan Gosling on the cutting edge of fashion with some kind of flair. Lorenzo may have never seen a Ryan Gosling movie, but he did appreciate the art of tailoring, spent a small fortune on his own wardrobe and subscribed to GQ. In another life, he and Damian might've been friends. Except Damian was always telling people how innovative and brilliant he was, though he had yet to do anything truly different or groundbreaking. It was the *look at me, look at me!* attitude Lorenzo despised, both ass-kissing and superior, laughing and glad-handing and ingratiating himself to the right people.

Lorenzo was one of the right people. However, when *he* was training, when *he* was a rising star, he'd did nothing to ingratiate himself to his superiors. Instead, he'd kept his head down, concentrated on his work, and let things flow from there. He'd listened to the chief residents, spent more time on the floor and in the OR than any other surgical resident, and, yes, was simply gifted, the same way Pavarotti had been born with a voice from God. Of course, the singer had to train, but a thousand other men could train as long and hard as Pavarotti and never sound like him.

And then there was his suture. Lorenzo had gone a step beyond, fulfilling the dream of many a physician by creating something that had never before existed in the medical world. Just after his residency, he designed a bio-responsive polymer suture that could detect inflammation or infection and release microdoses of antibiotics before these issues could be detected by bloodwork or radiology. He'd been thirty-three at the time (the same age as Jesus when he died, his grandmother had pointed out). The Intraweave suture had made him a star...and a very wealthy man. That, his gift in the OR and his excruciating standards made him legendary. He wasn't bragging. It was just true.

And, if he was being honest, it made him a little isolated among his peers. Small talk was a waste of his time, let alone golf or sailing. He didn't have children and didn't foresee any in his future (though he enjoyed holding Sofia's two children, as long as they were sleeping). He didn't think it would be fair to father a child he might only see a few hours a week, and he wasn't willing to cut back his schedule to change that. So, no kids. His siblings would have plenty, he was sure.

Ah. Damian had just clocked him. Too late. It was time for his talk. He went into the largest conference room to ensure everything was working. His lecture was on advanced trauma operative management. As usual, when he talked, it was standing-room only. The hotel staffer assured him everything was connected; the moderator gushed a moment and shook his hand, then introduced him. There was the usual applause, and he went to the podium. "Good afternoon," he said and began, his PowerPoint organized and clear. It had taken him days to put together.

The other surgeons typed away or recorded his talk, scribbled notes, nodding, murmuring. After the forty-five minutes had passed, he took questions until the hour ran out. "Thank you for your attention," he said, stepping down from the stage.

Immediately, Damian, his assistant trailing slightly behind him, approached.

"Lorenzo, great presentation. I'd love to discuss it more and get your take on a tricky septal myectomy I have next week. Can I buy you dinner? Chicago Chop House. I've heard it's the best. I have a reservation for two at eight o'clock, right, Carl?"

"That's right, Dr. Hughes," the assistant said. "The car service will pick you up at 7:45."

Lorenzo didn't answer. First of all, *Lorenzo?* He barely knew Damian Hughes and preferred that the younger man call him Dr. Santini until Lorenzo told him otherwise (which would be never). Second, Damian had presumed Lorenzo would accept the invitation to the iconic restaurant. And third, the showiness of having his assistant murmur affirmations, as if the details were too much for Damian to keep track of. Yes, yes, Lorenzo had just hired Winnie, but *he* wasn't three years out of residency. He was Dr. Satan, known and feared and, most of all, respected, not because he had an assistant but because he was a great surgeon.

"I already have plans with a group of senior surgeons, Dr. Hughes," he said. "But thank you." He kept his voice chilly, and saw the message land on Damian's face. *You haven't earned it yet.* And Lorenzo did have plans (not that he was looking forward to them and, in fact, was considering canceling). While he loved talking about surgery and medical issues, his fellow surgeons gushed about vacations and grandchildren and retirement.

But these were a necessary part of his job, both for him and the hospitals where he worked. He'd interact during conference hours. He'd suffer through a dinner. But whenever possible, he ordered room service or found a restaurant

far from the hotel where he could read without interruption.

His rejection of Damian Hughes did not go unmet.

Later that afternoon, Lorenzo sat in on a panel discussion about the readiness of chief residents. When asked by
the moderator if senior doctors were too hard on residents,
Lorenzo answered first. "Not hard enough, frankly," he said.
"If they can't handle the pressure of being criticized, they
certainly won't be able to handle a crisis in the OR. The kid-
glove approach is detrimental to their success, and, more
importantly, to patient outcomes."

Damian's hand shot up in the air. The moderator
walked down the aisle and handed him the microphone. He
stood, hand in one pocket of his lavender suit. "Dr. Santini,
I disagree. Mentoring and empathy have been shown time
and time again to be a more effective training method.
Insults and embarrassment should be a thing of the past."
There was a murmur of agreement from some of the
audience.

"I do not condone insults and embarrassment," Lorenzo
said. "You misunderstand. If a resident makes a mistake, I
am clear in correcting that mistake and suggesting further
education so said mistake is not made again."

"But you *do* insult and embarrass your residents,"
Damian said. "Your nickname is Dr. Satan."

A ripple of laughter rolled through the room.

"My residents go on to become some of the best
surgeons in the world," Lorenzo said, his words icy.
"Because I trained them. Next question, please?"

Of course Lorenzo was hard on his residents. When a
patient began hemorrhaging, when their heart rate dropped,
when a lung collapsed or they went into shock, when the
tumor was bigger than projected and clean margins meant

working half a millimeter from the aorta, a surgeon had to ignore everything else and focus. Treating a surgical trainee like a fragile snowflake did not serve them. That *was* mentoring.

Also, the Dr. Satan reference was juvenile. Granted, Lorenzo was somewhat proud of it, but it should stay in the applicable hospitals—not something to be made into a joke by a younger surgeon in front of their colleagues.

Irritating. When the day finally ended and all the talks were done and groups of people stood in the lobby waiting for their rides, Lorenzo walked briskly through the crowd, nodding here and there, saying "thank you" when told his talk was informative, greeting a few people by name. He texted the organizer of the dinner and said unfortunately he would have to cancel.

Getting back to his room felt like getting a reprieve from the governor at ten minutes to midnight. Even if his room was not a suite.

EIGHT

WINNIE

With Lorenzo at his conference, Winnie stayed in Chatham, the house was essentially the nicest Airbnb she could never have afforded. She checked in with the carpenter who was working on the deck stairs (she'd offered him twenty percent more if he made the job a priority, since carpenters were in high demand on the Cape). She also made sure the landscaper knew not to cut back the beach plums and would mow the grass on the diagonal per Lorenzo's request.

Apparently, he'd been pleased enough with her work so far to expand her duties. He gave her access to his email so she could cull the junk and say no to any requests that "waste my time"—anything not incredibly prestigious, that was. She also printed out his fan mail, which was a bit of a surprise to her...gushing thanks from patients and their families, suck-up notes from residents who wanted to work under him, compliments from his colleagues. She printed those out and sorted them into color-coded folders so he could look at them when he wanted to (if ever). She also organized his calendar (and hers) with hour-before alerts for every meeting, surgery or engagement. In addition to his daily runs (sometimes done before it was light out), Lorenzo belonged to a fancy gym in Boston, one that was open twenty-four hours a day. At his instructions, she found four ninety-minute gaps in his schedule each week so he could stay fit.

It was satisfying. He had an impressive life, she was learning. All the hype seemed true. And at the end of those days, while he was in Boston or traveling, she sat on the deck, walked on the beach, then sat on the deck some more and read. The big blond dog was often out, galumphing down the beach, rolling in the sand, barking at waves. Winnie loved playing with her, as the dog was pure joy (and wet fur, and sand, and loved to shake the minute Winnie was close enough). She had taken to calling the dog Fluffina Laroux, for obvious reasons. So far, she had yet to see a human with the dog, and Fluffina had quickly learned that Winnie had bacon treats. She didn't seem particularly well trained, though she was very smart. Winnie taught her to sit, lie down and fetch, though Fluffina wanted Winnie to chase her and romp before surrendering the stick. As Winnie headed back, the dog would follow her to the beach stairs, then sit, her head cocked hopefully, waiting to be invited into the house. "Sorry, honey," Winnie said. "I don't think the boss would appreciate that."

Whoever owned the dog was lucky. Fluffina was good company...sometimes the only creature Winnie spoke to while at Lorenzo's, in person at least. On the rare day Fluffina wasn't on the beach, Winnie felt a real pang of missing her. Wondered about her owners, and if she got enough attention.

Winnie had never been the kind of person who'd had friends. When you grew up in a big family, maybe you didn't need friends as much. In school, there were the kids she sat with during lunch, but as far as sleepovers and giggles, not really, no. Within the family, Lark and Addison were welded together, psychically connected to the point where they spoke in unison or wore their hair the same way without planning. Harlow was eight years older than Winnie, and it was only in the past little while that she'd stopped treating Winnie like she was six. Robbie, when he wasn't making fun of her or another family member, had dozens of male friends, and until recently, shared a sticky, foul-smelling house with four or five of them. Over the summer, he and Rosie had bought a pretty little house in Eastham down by Boat Meadow, one of the prettiest bayside beaches on the Cape.

Her parents were great...seriously, no complaints unless Winnie thought really hard. Sure, she'd felt lost in the shuffle, but they'd had five kids in nine years. She understood. They liked her (in addition to loving her), often called her their most sensible child, the one who could handle a crisis without a flicker of an eyelash. Harlow might freeze when surprised, and Addie fainted at the sight of blood. Lark was a weeper, Robbie too irreverent. Winnie was the one who got shit done. It was a point of pride.

But there weren't many crises where her skill set was needed, and being slightly invisible was a comfortable place to be. Addie had once told her she was probably on the spectrum, but Winnie thought she just liked solitude more than most. She owned a paddleboard, grew flowers in her tiny garden, read and listened to books, and loved to bake. She didn't drink much and, unlike her grandfather and Robbie, had never tried weed. She didn't have a house big enough to host family events, and other than her birthday, didn't do much that warranted celebration. In other words, she was a wallpaper sort of person. Every family had one.

And so, one of the reasons she had loved, then hated, Mitchell was because he'd made her feel like...well, like someone else. Someone sparkling, someone who lit up a room (though that quality was one of the red flags for murder, according to *Dateline*). Mitchell had made her feel special, and Winnie honestly wasn't. She was fine. She was dependable. She was honest and hardworking. She did not sparkle.

And then there was just the whole *being part of a couple* thing. Everyone in her family—including Grandpop—had found someone. Even Cynthia, their sour-faced cousin, had found her person and fallen in love. Winnie had heard all the phrases people said since she was seventeen. *Are you seeing someone? Don't worry, your time will come. Love happens when you least expect it. Plenty of guys out there. Have you tried online dating? Have you gotten off the apps? Let me think if I know some nice single guy. Hm. I don't.*

The world was built for couples, and while Winnie was not a romantic, there had been a dark little corner of her heart that had hoped someday, she'd meet someone great. That was the sucker punch of it all. She really thought she had. Hard to accept she hadn't sensed Mitchell-Tanner was lying. Harder still to admit she missed feeling so...adored.

On Sunday, she drove from Chatham to Wellfleet to check in with her parents before her meeting with Robbie and Rosie. She assured Mom and Dad she was fine, liked her job, and then went to her sister's bookstore, where she was meeting the happy couple. They were there, and Harlow was just closing up.

"Hi, sweetie!" Harlow said. "Take as long as you need.

Just make sure Grandpop doesn't lock himself in again, okay? He got stuck inside last week and slept here, then tapped on the window until Lillie Silva saw him and called me."

"Left his phone at home?"

"Correct." They both smiled.

"I'll make sure he's safe and sound when I leave. How are Grady and Luna?"

Harlow's face softened. "They're great. It's family fun night, so we're going to the beach to build sandcastles and then to Mac's for lobster rolls."

Familial bliss. "And Matthew? Mom said he's staying for Christmas?"

"He is! The wedding is three days after his last exam, so he'll come out for that and stay." Harlow's face glowed at the thought of her son, who was now in college. "Okay, gotta run. You doing okay, honey?"

"Right as rain."

Harlow tilted her head and looked at her. "If you want to talk, I'm always here, Winnie."

"I know. And thanks." She did know. She just didn't like picking her emotional scabs in front of people. She went into the main room of the bookstore and found Robbie, Rosie and Grandpop in the sitting area—R and R on the couch, Grandpop in the wingchair across from them.

"Winnie! How beautiful and refreshing you are, like a bowl of oranges! Or a bouquet of daisies! Or a flock of bluebirds!"

"Grandpop, you are the best," she said. "Lark told me you rescued a squirrel from a tree this morning."

"Now, now, Winnie," her grandfather said, his blue eyes twinkling. "He looked very much like a cat, and you know how I love cats."

"If you fall out of a tree, I'll have to be Robbie's best man, so be careful, okay?" She kissed his head, then turned to Robbie and Rosie. "Ready to talk nuptials?"

"I'm already working on my speech," Grandpop said. "Trying to keep it under half an hour."

Rosie grinned at Winnie. "It'll kick ass, Grandpop," Robbie said.

"Shoot for ten minutes, Grandpop," Winnie said.

"Are you kidding?" Robbie said. "Take as long as you need, Grandpop. I want to hear how wonderful I am. The favorite grandchild, your best friend, your role model…"

"His gummy supplier. Robbie, you'll get plenty of attention, okay? Have you thought any more about the ceremony? I sent you some readings and poems and all that. And some samples of vows."

"We want to write our own," Rosie said.

"Nice," Winnie answered. "Always so meaningful. Robbie, I'll write yours so you don't embarrass yourself."

"Hey! When it comes to Rosie, I'm Ed Sheeran."

"Ew," Rosie and Winnie said at the same time.

For the next hour, they discussed the logistics of the ceremony. Flower arrangements—"the pretty kind," Robbie requested—special cocktails (and mocktails, since Rosie, Dad and Nicole didn't drink). Dresses for the flower girls. A toast from Rosie's dad, grace by Mom. Winnie had scheduled their cake tasting, and Mr. Wolfe would be choosing the wine.

There would be warm brownies served after cake, an ice cream sundae bar, sandwiches at midnight. For favors, each guest would receive a gift bag containing hand-blown ornaments from Sydenstricker Glass, a jar of local honey, chocolates from Chequessett Chocolates and a candle that allegedly smelled like the Cape air. "How about a pony? Should everyone get a pony?" Robbie asked.

"Dad wants it to be memorable. He'll have some of his colleagues and clients there."

"Any celebrities?" Grandpop asked. "I wonder if he knows Helen Mirren. I find her *quite* attractive."

"You have a girlfriend," Winnie reminded him. "But yeah, Rosie, would anyone need security?"

"Uncle Jeff is the only actor coming, I think," Rosie said.

"Which Jeff is that?" Winnie asked.

"Jeff Bridges."

"*The Big Lebowski* is one of my *favorite* movies!" Grandpop exclaimed. "I wonder if he'd let me take a selfie with him."

"He would," Rosie said. "And he won't need security, don't worry. Maybe Tom and Rita, but I think Dad said they'd be in New Zealand. We can hang out in LA when we visit Dad."

"How did you trick her into marrying you again?" Winnie asked.

"Just my good looks and lover-man skills."

She winced. "Our grandfather is right there."

"He's sleeping," Robbie said. Winnie glanced at Grandpop to confirm.

"Anything else, Winneria?" Robbie asked. "My brain is shutting down."

"I think we're good," she said, looking at her iPad. "Rosie, you have a fitting in Boston next week."

"Yep! Will you come? Lark and Harlow will be there. Addison is a maybe."

"I'll see if I can," Winnie said. "Thank you for including me."

"Of course, hon," she said, giving her a one-armed hug.

"Oh, you should swing by and see our house! We're gutting the kitchen and would love to hear what you think"

Winnie watched as they left, hand in hand, laughing at something. Both of them had so much energy, were so outgoing and happy, like puppies. Adorable, but exhausting, all that adoration.

"How are you doing, my dear?" Grandpop asked, waking abruptly. "Our family is filled with happy couples. It must feel a bit tiring occasionally."

The man might mistake a squirrel for a cat, but he was a little too smart sometimes. "Eh. I think I'm better off alone."

"Come now. I know you were quite smitten."

She felt her throat tighten and didn't answer.

"Tell your old grandfather," he said. "I can keep a secret. Or I'll just forget what you said. Either way, unburden yourself, sweetheart."

She shrugged. "Well, it's...I mean, I never thought I'd be in *love*-love, you know? And that was okay. I figured I wasn't the type."

"But then you found yourself exactly the type," he said.

She nodded, ordering herself not to cry. "Yeah. Sure. But the guy I loved was a liar. A really good liar who had no problem cheating on the mother of his children or jerking me around. Long story short, I think the universe is telling me to stick to the sidelines where I work best."

"It's telling you you're human, my dear. That's the only thing the universe is saying. People wear masks, and it takes some time to see beneath them. It doesn't mean it's your destiny to be alone."

"I think it is. And I'm okay with that. Anyway, Grandpop, I should go. I have to drive back to Chatham."

"There are some people who can make us feel like we're an entirely different sort of person," Grandpop said, covering her hand with his own. His skin was crepey and thin, but his hand was warm. "And then there are those who make us feel that we're perfect just as we are. My guess is that the former was your experience, am I right?"

She gave a reluctant nod. All that...happiness, that lightness and laughter...It was as if she'd been a version of herself she didn't know existed. "I'm not the most...magnetic person in the world. So when he noticed me..." She swallowed. "I was flattered."

"No!" Grandpop almost shouted. "You *should* expect someone to notice you, darling girl! You're lovely and unique. If someone doesn't see that, it's because he's the wrong person. The right person will know your value."

"So far, Grandpop, you're the only one."

He laughed. "You're still very young."

"Not really. I'm almost thirty-three."

"Just out of *infancy*! Don't worry, sweetheart. Your old grandpop knows a thing or two. Why, just yesterday when I was cleaning out the gutters—"

"Grandpop! What do we say about ladders?"

"Oh, pish," he said. "When I was cleaning out the gutters...well, I nearly did fall, you know, but luckily, I grabbed the cornice and saved myself in the nick of time. Anyway, what I meant to say was that as I was clinging there, waiting for gravity to make up its mind, I found myself thinking that you're my only grandchild not matched just yet. And I hope to see you happily ensconced in a wonderful relationship before I die."

"All the more reason for me to stay single, Grandpop, if that's your line in the sand. I have to go now."

"All right, sweetheart. I love you."

"Love you, too."

It would be a relief, she thought, to get back to

Chatham, to the empty, beautiful house...Lorenzo was in Boston for the next two days, so she could pretend she lived in that beautiful, sterile house and fantasize about what she'd do to warm it up. The couch was coming tomorrow—a long, sumptuous velvet thing the color of red wine. She could watch a movie there and put the unused television to work.

She got off Route 6 in Eastham and headed toward Boat Meadow to see Robbie and Rosie's house. Rosie worked as a location scout for movies, and it either paid very well, or her dad was made of money, because the view was incredible. It was low tide, and the mud flats stretched out a half mile or so. She got out and walked down the sandy little path that wound through the sea grass to the house where her formerly feckless brother would be living.

Little Robbie had done okay after all, she thought with a smile. A good job, the girl he'd loved since he was an adolescent, and now this place to come home to each night. She peeked in the windows. Lots of work to be done, but it would be a stunner, she was sure.

She walked back to her car, hearing the piping plovers and orange-billed oystercatchers as they darted about. Maybe she'd sit on one of the benches and watch the sunset. That kind of thing soothed the soul.

Then she heard a familiar laugh, and the squeal of a child.

The Johnson family was here. All five of them. She recognized Mitchell's curly hair, his laughing voice. Blakelee was wearing a colorful summery dress, and the three kids were frolicking and prancing at their sides.

They looked like the fake photos they use in frames—the wholesome, fun family, love shimmering all around them. The kind of photo that showed you what you were missing.

Enough. Mitchell-Tanner had taken enough of her brain and heart space today.

She went back to her car, careful not to slink or cower, then headed down the dirt road, turned onto Bridge Road and headed for Chatham. She would do what she always did. Be productive. Be useful. Try not to think too hard about her broken heart and how it had felt to be loved...even if that love had not been real.

LORENZO HAD RETURNED from his conference, but he told her he'd be in Boston, so Winnie chose to stay put in Chatham. Fluffina needed her, and while she could ostensibly work from her tiny house in Wellfleet, she wanted to stay here for the time being.

Every day, Lorenzo sent her a brief email telling her what he needed. Her job was about sixty percent personal, forty percent professional, though that was growing as he began to trust her organizational skills and prompt response times. She might drive into Boston to do some grocery shopping, unpack things, make sure the house was pristine. She proofread one of his articles, found three entire typos and marked them. Watered the plants on his terrace, scheduled his monthly and wildly expensive haircut. She had his Persian carpets cleaned by a specialty rug cleaner, hired a window washer, though the building super was supposed to have done that, and inspected the house after the cleaners had been through to make sure they hadn't missed something. She was a clean freak, after all.

In Chatham, Lorenzo asked her to furnish two of the

guest bedrooms on the lower level, including her own, so she'd been buying sheets, curtains and duvets, then scouring antique stores and Facebook Marketplace for authentic mid-century modern accents and furniture. It was wicked fun, and also perhaps another glimpse into his personal life. His house had five bedrooms. He probably hadn't bought such a big house to stay empty. Either he wanted to have guests, or he wanted a big family.

Speaking of his family, Winnie found she also had access to his photos file. She was fairly sure he wasn't aware of this, but it didn't stop her from looking. There was a shared family folder; otherwise, Lorenzo didn't seem the type to whip out his phone and take a picture of a view, or meal, or hotel room. He didn't seem to have taken any photos at all. Maybe he was old-school and used film, but his computer contained only those uploaded by his siblings and parents.

The family photos were almost familiar, the type her own family took—birthdays and Christmas, kids dressed up for Halloween, parents beaming. Isabella and Sofia seemed close—lots of photos of the two of them, often with one of Sofia's children. Plenty of Dante looking wicked hot, pun intended, in Boston firefighting gear or in front of a firehouse. There were fewer of Lorenzo—mostly at weddings and the christenings of William and Lucy, Sofia's kids. He was in maybe one in fifteen of the photos in the shared folder, and that gave her a pang.

She paused at a picture of Lorenzo holding his nephew, then a newborn. He was staring intently at the baby's face, and the baby was looking right back at him. Both of them were in profile, and Winnie could almost feel their connection. William could not have been more than two months old. Another photo showed him kissing Lucy's forehead, the baby swathed in pink.

On impulse, she clicked on a few photos and air-dropped them to her own phone. She'd get them printed and framed. Even Lorenzo's chilly heart would love that.

A FEW DAYS LATER, a chilly October rain blew against the windows of Lorenzo's house, and the wind gusted in great slaps, sudden and unpredictable. A classic wild and rainy Cape Cod day, Winnie thought, and good for indoor projects. She was rearranging the massive bookshelves that took up one wall of his living room, trying to stick to subject material, though ninety percent were medical-related. She had a spreadsheet going by title and author—there were at least two hundred books—so if Lorenzo couldn't find something, he could just reference the list. In addition to medicine, Lorenzo seemed to be interested in underground infrastructure—he had books on subways, water systems, tunnels and cables. In the entire collection, she found only four works of fiction—*Cutting for Stone* by Abraham Verghese; *The Crucible* by Arthur Miller; *The English Patient* by Michael Ondaatje; and *The Plague* by Albert Camus. Cheery stuff.

Every so often, she turned the books to lie flat to break up the imposing collection and added some visual interest—a big twist of driftwood Fluffina had brought her this morning, smooth as polished marble from its time in the sea. A painting she'd made herself, mostly smears of color from the last time Mom had tried to give her an art lesson. The colors were pretty, at any rate. At Wayne's Antiques in Brewster, her favorite place to poke around, she'd found an abstract metal thingie—a semi-circle with a ball on one end—that she thought would fit in. In the closet of one of the downstairs bedrooms, she'd found a cobalt-blue glass bowl. And, one night on whimsy, she ordered him a gift—a brass reproduction of Houdon's flayed man statue, which was both beautiful and horrific. It looked great on the shelf, and Winnie wondered if he'd notice.

She had a Spotify jazz playlist going on...stuff with melodies, not the stuff that sounded like Imogen on the recorder. Between that and the storm outside, she didn't hear anyone pull up the driveway, so when the door opened, she whirled around, Flayed Man in hand in case it was an intruder (thanks, *Dateline*).

It wasn't a murderer. It was Lark and Dante. "Hey!" she said, her heart squeezing with love. She hadn't seen her sister in at least two weeks.

"Did you think I was Lorenzo?" Dante asked, nodding at the raised statue. She smiled, put it down, and accepted a hug from her brother-in-law. "Are you happy it's not?"

"I have no complaints about my employer," she said.

"You sure? Do I need to punch him yet?" Dante asked.

"Winnie can punch for herself," Lark said, smiling as she hugged her. "Gosh, you look so pretty today, Winnie. Really. Very healthy."

"Those gorgeous Smith sisters. How did I get so lucky?" Dante asked.

"A blip in the matrix," Winnie said. "Lorenzo isn't here, I'm sorry to say. If you were coming to see him, that is."

"We were coming to see you," Lark said. "I texted you."

"Oh. Sorry I missed it."

"That's okay. How do you like staying here? Isn't it the prettiest house?"

"It really is."

"I'm guessing those flowers and houseplants are your touch," Lark said. "Very pretty. Where are you sleeping?"

"Downstairs. I have a little suite."

Dante's phone buzzed. "Hey, Robbie," he said. "I'm standing here with half of your sisters. What's up? Yeah. No, we're at my brother's, actually. Sure. Come on over, it's a wicked cool house. Texting you the address." He looked at Winnie and Lark. "Robbie and Rosie just finished cake-tasting. They're coming over."

Winnie felt a pang of protectiveness. "Um...maybe let's run this past Lorenzo," she said.

"Nah," Dante said. "His casa, mi casa, as the saying goes. He won't mind."

Winnie thought he might mind very much. But he was in Boston, and he'd never said she couldn't have people over, especially when it was his brother doing the inviting. "Okay, then. Can I get you something to drink?"

Twenty minutes later, the five of them were sitting in the living room. Winnie had set out a tray of cheese and crackers, grapes and sliced apples, a little thrilled at the chance to play hostess and use Lorenzo's beautiful stuff. Winnie'd made herself and Lark a gin and tonic, Robbie and Dante were drinking beer, and Rosie had a tonic and cranberry juice with a sprig of rosemary that Winnie had added for flair.

"So this doesn't trigger you or anything?" Winnie asked, pointing to the alcohol.

"Oh, no," Rosie said. "I didn't drink because I liked the taste of wine. I drank to get shit-faced. Guzzle vodka from a bottle at ten a.m., that kind of thing. My recovery is solid, my therapist is great, and I've never been so happy."

"So impressive," Lark said. "We're all really proud of you, Rosie."

"Well. Robbie is my rock."

"First time anyone's ever said those words," Winnie said. Robbie gave her the finger, then leaned over and kissed his fiancée.

"Please don't," Winnie said. "Happy couples are *my* trigger. Stop making heart eyes, you four."

"You doing okay with all that?" Dante asked. "The married boyfriend situation?"

"Yes. Good talk."

"Winipedia," Robbie said, "my bachelor party is coming, and I want you to come. If Grandpop wasn't my best man, it would totally be you. You're basically a guy. I mean, I think of you as my brother."

"That's the nicest thing you've ever said to me, Robbie." She wouldn't have minded being best woman, but she also loved that he asked Grandpop.

"Don't get used to it. Grandpop can't plan what to eat for lunch, let alone a bachelor party, so Austin's taking the reins. The party bus will pick you up."

"Are your other sisters invited?" Lark said.

"Absolutely not," said Robbie. "Just Winster the Spinster."

"And just like that, you're an idiot again," Winnie said. "But yes, I'm free, and I can't wait. Tell Austin to call me if he needs help."

At that moment, the front door open, and there stood Lorenzo, dressed in a raincoat and suit. "What are you doing here?" he asked. "Did someone die?"

"Hey, Lorenzo!" Dante said, jumping up and going to hug his brother. "We just dropped in to see Winnie, and Robbie and Rosie were in the neighborhood, so we asked them to come over."

"I see."

Winnie could also see that Lorenzo was a little off-balance with the company. Chances were high he'd been working all weekend and had wanted the peace and quiet of home. After all, there was nothing as soul-soothing as a Cape Cod storm.

"Lorenzo, how you doing, man?" Robbie asked. "We were just talking about my bachelor party. November fifteenth, okay? You have to come."

"Oh…I…I'm not sure I'm free."

"Is he, Window? I mean, you're his PA, right?"

"I am. I can check later," she said.

"Check now. We're practically related, Lorenzo. I'd love to have you hang with us," Robbie said.

At Lorenzo's nod, Winnie looked at her phone. "At the moment, you are free," she said.

"Awesome!" Robbie said. "You can keep Dante company, because he won't know most of the guys, either. That's great. Thanks, man."

"I…yes. You're welcome," Lorenzo said. "I'm sure it will be fun."

Winnie guessed he'd schedule something important for that day to have a good excuse to cancel. Then again, maybe he did want to go. He sure didn't seem to have an active social life, just dinners with colleagues.

"Hello, Lark. Hello, ah, Rosie." Lorenzo gave a slight bow toward the women.

"Nice to see you again," Rosie said. "And yes, we've met before."

"Of course."

"Can I get you a drink, boss?" Winnie asked. "Brennevin, maybe?"

"Ah, sure. Thank you."

For the next ninety minutes, Winnie watched as

Lorenzo politely asked questions of Rosie, checked in with Lark about work and generally stayed quiet about himself. He sipped his drink, had once piece of cheese and four grapes. When Rosie complimented him on the house, he offered her a tour. In other words, he was quietly, politely gracious. She wondered if he hated every minute, or if, as it seemed, he might have been enjoying himself.

When the other two couples had left, Winnie cleared the cheese board, put their glasses in the dishwasher and tidied up. "Sorry about that," she said. "I didn't think I should turn your brother away."

"No. You shouldn't. Why was *your* brother here, though?"

"He was in the area, and Dante asked him if he wanted to stop by. If you don't want me to have people over, just say the word."

"It's fine."

"You sure?"

"Yes. A little warning would've been nice, though."

"You told me you were staying in Boston."

"I thought I shared my location with you so you could see if I had changed plans."

Yes. He had done that, at her suggestion. "Sorry. Maybe a text next time?"

"That's reasonable. However, if you're here in my home, assume you're on the clock," he said. "You're welcome to host parties at your own home in Wellfleet."

"This was unplanned, and it was *your* brother who invited *my* brother here."

"My private time is very important to me."

"You just *said* it was fine." She felt the irritation rising, coloring her cheeks.

"And it *is*." His voice was tight now. "But you could've

also texted me, Winnie, and alerted me to the fact that I had company."

"And I *would* have, except you told me this morning you'd be staying in Boston."

"Well, my plans changed, and as I just said, my down time is very important to me."

"I get it, Lorenzo. Jesus-in-the-garden vibe. Sorry we ruined it."

"You didn't ruin it. But your family is relentless with their bonding, aren't they?"

"We are. Hashtag proud, hashtag family."

He glanced at the bookcase. "You reorganized."

She smiled. "I did." She opened her laptop. "Check this out. Every book is cross-referenced by subject, title, and author for your convenience. Looks nice, doesn't it?"

He looked at the screen, then back at the wall of books. Said nothing.

"I'll interpret your silence as admiration," she said.

"Where did this come from?" he asked. He walked over to the photo of him holding William and picked it up. "I've never seen it before."

"I printed some photos and framed them. There are a few more scattered around the house," she said. "Feel free to rearrange them, of course."

"Thank you. I should've...Where did you find them?"

"On your computer." She waited for him to chide her for looking in files he had not told her to.

He didn't. He set the photo back down and looked at the shelves again. "Is that The Flayed Man?" he asked.

She grinned. "It is. It's a gift. Boss Appreciation Day."

"Is that a real holiday?"

"I think I just made it up," she said.

He almost smiled. "I love it." He touched the blue glass

bowl. "This was my grandmother's," he said. "Sometimes she'd let me eat ice cream from it. And where did you find this?" He indicated her painting.

"Oh. That's the work of an up-and-coming artist from the Outer Cape."

He glanced at her. "You?"

"Yes! How did you know?"

"It's extremely symmetrical. Don't quit your day job." He was smiling at her. She almost had to fact-check his face, but yes, that was a smile. "Thank you. It looks very... thoughtful."

"You're welcome." He didn't say anything else, and for a second, they just looked at each other, the faint roar of the waves the only sound.

Invite me to stay.

The thought came as a surprise. She *could* stay, of course—she had a room downstairs—but suddenly, she thought she should leave, although why, she wasn't sure.

"Okay," she said. "I think I'll head back to Wellfleet and watch the storm from my place."

"Drive safely."

Drat. If he had said she shouldn't drive in the rain, she would've caved. "I always do."

He glanced at her, and his mouth moved a fraction at the corners. "Text me when you get there so I know you made it."

Go figure.

He picked up the photo of him and William again and studied it, and Winnie could tell he was no longer thinking about her. It was oddly disappointing.

"Have a good night, Lorenzo."

He was still looking at the photo when she left the house.

NINE

LORENZO

Lorenzo had asked Winnie to come to Boston.

It had been four days since he'd seen her last, since he'd seen the photos she had framed for him, the inexplicably perfect additions she made to his house. The curved little statue was a Tom Bennett sculpture; she'd bought it for $75 on the Cape, but it was worth closer to a thousand. A piece of driftwood, a martini glass filled with white stones, an embroidered red cushion against his white pillows. The woman who'd overseen the interior decorating of his home could've learned a thing or two from Winnie Smith. It wasn't her taste per se...it was that he loved everything. That he would've chosen everything, if he'd had the time and inclination.

But it was the family photos that really got to him.

Every time he saw one, his hypothalamus passed his pituitary gland a little oxytocin into his bloodstream. In addition to the photo of him meeting William for the first time, there was one of him and Lucy, a picture of his parents on their wedding day (where she had found that, he had no idea). There a casual shot of him and Dante last year, one of the few times where they looked like brothers, not distant relatives, the both of them leaning on the deck railing here, their faces turned toward each other in conversation, neither particularly smiling, but both of them relaxed. There was a photo of him dancing with Noni at Sofia's wedding...Noni had wobbled to her feet, and Lorenzo could still feel the pleasure of making his grandmother smile and laugh, hearing her Italian words telling him she was too old for this. Some part of him had known it would be the last time they'd have a chance for something fun. Sure enough, Noni had died a few weeks later.

In short, it was incredibly nice, having a personal assistant. He hadn't realized she'd be quite *so* personal, digging into his family photos and rearranging things, but oddly enough, he didn't mind. The flowers. The bread. The rearranged and artfully ordered bookcases.

His phone dinged—the doorman letting him know that a Ms. Smith was here to see him. Send her up, thanks, he wrote back. A moment later, Winnie walked into his apartment, dressed in boring clothes—beige pants, navy sweater, small hoop earrings, and sensible brown shoes.

"You look like a nun," he said.

"Nice to see you, too, Dr. Satan." She seemed unperturbed. "Actually, since I've been working for you for a month now, can I just call you Satan?"

He ignored the request, still frowning at her frumpy clothes. "As my assistant, I'd like you to dress more professionally. Especially as you'll be coming with me to San Francisco."

Her eyes widened. "Excuse me?"

"Is that a problem?" he asked. "I believe you said attending conferences would not be a problem, and I asked if this time frame was free. We leave at seven in the morning." She *had* said she was free, and he'd be irked if she begged off. This conference was the most prestigious of the year—he'd be giving a presentation on potential complications when using techniques for abdominal surgery. He'd also agreed to sit on a panel or two, though he liked that less. "Winnie? Will that be a problem?"

"I just wish you'd mentioned it before now."

"I did."

"No, you didn't." She fished out her phone and read, "'Is your calendar free Monday through Thursday?' Me: 'Yes.' End of conversation."

"Oh." Guess he hadn't mentioned it specifically. "Well, you're free, so I'd like to take you to the conference."

"No, that's fine. I just didn't realize I'd be away for a few days. I'll have to drive back and pack, then make it to Logan by seven a.m. I guess I also have to book myself a ticket."

"I had my travel agent do it. I'm firing him, by the way, so expect that to become one of your duties. So you have no clothes or toiletries?"

"Not with me, no."

"In the future, you should keep some things here. For now—" He paused. She didn't exactly dress to impress. He glanced at his Apple watch. He had allocated two hours for their meeting, but he was a surgeon, and multitasking came easily. "Let's go. I can fill you in on what I'll be doing at the conference and what I need from you while we get you some appropriate clothing."

"We're going shopping?"

"You just said you have nothing with you. Bring your iPad."

One hundred and seventeen minutes and several thousand dollars later, Winnie had a work wardrobe appropriate for the PA of a renowned surgeon. A breathless clerk from one of the posh stores on Newbury Street had helped select something she called a "capsule wardrobe," and Winnie had tried things on without complaint. A white suit, a black suit, a black dress, a white shirt, gray pants, black pants, black sweater, white sweater. Two pairs of shoes, a pair of boots. The clerk was folding the clothing now, and Winnie was back in her sad, nun-like outfit. She took out her hair elastic, smoothed her slightly disheveled hair back, and refastened her ponytail.

"Does all this work for you?" he asked, indicating the array of bags on the counter.

"Sure. I could've gone to Marshall's and gotten essentially the same thing for about two hundred dollars. But if dressing women is your kink, well, I work for you, Satan."

He narrowed his eyes, an unfamiliar sense of...something...uncurling in his stomach. Something not unpleasant. He liked that she sparred with him, wasn't intimidated by him, took things in stride. He liked it a lot. "I want you to look like the successful woman you are."

She raised her eyebrows in surprise, then her cheeks flushed an attractive pink. "Well. Thank you."

"A perk of the job. I should have thought of it before. I'll give you a wardrobe allowance."

"This is plenty," she said. "Please."

"I bought your sister some dresses when she worked for me," he said.

"Oh, I know. We heard all about that. You have great taste."

Lorenzo glanced at her, but there didn't seem to be a subtext there. "Thank you."

Once again, Winnie looked plain yet tidy. He could see her resemblance to Lark, though Winnie's face was less... dewy and sentimental somehow. Lark wore her heart on her sleeve; Winnie had hers firmly tucked away, a quality he appreciated.

Lorenzo paid and took the bags. He glanced at his watch. 5:04. It was early, but they hadn't really discussed the conference. "Would you like to have dinner?" he surprised himself by asking.

"Sure," she said easily. "I'm starving."

They walked the few blocks to Grill 23, where Lorenzo ate once a month when he needed meat, which he guiltily loved, though he otherwise kept his diet to chicken, eggs, tofu, and fish for protein.

"Very nice to see you again, Dr. Santini," said Mateo, the maître d'. "Good evening, miss. May I store those bags for you?"

"Thank you," Lorenzo said, handing them over. Mateo then led them to a table overlooking the street, handed them the wine list and menus, and told them to enjoy their dinners.

"You're a regular here, I take it?" Winnie asked, opening the menu. Her eyes widened. Hazel, he noted. Greenish-grayish-goldish. "Oof," she said softly. Yes. The prices were steep, but the food was well worth it.

"I'm paying, of course. This is a business dinner." He already knew what he was having—tomahawk dry-aged steak, baked potato (hold the sour cream and butter) and Brussels sprouts (hold the parmesan). A glass of California cabernet sauvignon.

When the waiter came by, Winnie ordered the roast chicken and a glass of pinot grigio, which made Lorenzo cringe inside. It was more like grape juice than actual wine.

"You can order whatever you want," he said as the waiter left.

"I did," she said.

"Both of those things are the least expensive things on the menu."

"I like roast chicken."

He remembered how much Lark had loved to order when she'd been his companion the summer his sister got married. Granted, she'd been a starving resident then, but she'd also enjoyed running up the tab.

"Are you close with your sisters?" he asked.

"I am. And Robbie, too. He and I shared a room for years. Are you close with yours?"

He considered the question. "Somewhat. Sofia and I get along easily. She's closest in age to me. Isabella is a nurse, so we have some professional things in common." Not many, he thought, still irked years later that Izzy hadn't accepted his offer to pay for medical school. "Dante and I are getting closer, now that he's settled down. He comes by from time to time."

"That's nice." She sipped some water and looked at the flowers on the table, touching one petal.

What was nice, he thought, was having a conversation with someone who wasn't digging for more answers. Another difference from Lark.

"Do you have a partner, Winnie?" he asked. "Someone who minds you leaving for days at a time?"

"No," she said. "I don't." Her cheeks flushed again, a less pretty shade this time, indicating that her sympathetic nervous system had been triggered more dramatically than when he'd complimented her in the store. The vasodilation released erythrocytes subcutaneously on the face, which had more capillary loops than anywhere else in the body. Such increased blood flow would aid in a fight-or-flight situation.

Interesting.

"I did have someone," she said abruptly. "We broke up."

"Recently?"

"Yes."

He paused. This *was* his brother's wife's sister, so he supposed he should say something kind. "Would you like to talk about it?"

"God, no."

Again, appreciation flared. The server arrived with their wine, and Winnie took a healthy slug.

Over dinner, Lorenzo outlined what he wanted her to do at the conference, which was essentially make sure that everything ran smoothly. "People tend to want my time," he said. "I don't have a lot to give."

"Be your Rottweiler. Got it."

He almost smiled. "Yes. Also, I never trust the technical staff at these things," he said. "Do you know how to connect a PowerPoint presentation to a screen?"

"I do," she said.

"And how do you know that?"

She gave him a slightly irritated look. "Because a lot of parties feature that kind of thing...kids over the years, first dates, all that." She took the last bite of her chicken, wiped her mouth, and set down her fork. "That was delicious. Thank you."

"Would you like dessert?" he asked.

"Yes, but you don't like dessert, so we can get the check. I have to pack, anyway. Do you have a suitcase I can borrow? I just thought of that."

"Yes, I do."

"Would you like me to pack for you?" she asked.

"Oh. No, that's fine."

"I am your personal assistant, after all," she said. "When I was a teenager, I worked at a clothing store in Wellfleet. I can fold clothes perfectly. And I've seen boxer shorts before. I'll bet you have some things to review before tomorrow morning."

He felt his mouth tug at one corner. "I...all right, then. Sure." It felt oddly intimate, but as she said, that was her job.

He paid the bill, gathered up her bags, and together they walked home through the Public Garden, past the duckling statues, then onto Beacon Street. They didn't talk.

"You have two very beautiful homes," Winnie said as they went up the stairs of his apartment building. It *was* beautiful, built in the late 1800s, red brick and granite.

"Thank you," he said. She had yet to stay over here, so he showed her to the guest room, got a spare suitcase and set his own on his bed, then pulled out the clothes he'd be wearing—three suits, five shirts, four ties, five pairs of socks, two pairs of linen trousers and two sweaters for traveling, plus his running clothes and sneakers. And yes, his boxers. He kept a toiletry bag packed at all times, since he didn't like to have to wonder if he'd forgotten anything.

Then he went down the hall to the library, opened his laptop, and went over his notes once more. As he did, he could hear Winnie moving around down the hall, opening doors and drawers, humming as she did.

It was a surprisingly nice sound.

TEN

Winnie had slept like the dead in the exquisitely comfortable bed in Lorenzo's guest room. After they'd come back from dinner last night, she'd gone down to the nearest CVS and bought herself the necessary toiletries and a small case for the same. Then she packed their suitcases while Lorenzo did whatever Lorenzo did in the evenings. (Hint: he was in the den, and he was quiet.) She didn't see him again until she walked into the kitchen at 6:00 a.m.

"Good morning," he said.

"Good morning," she returned, and wheeled his suitcase toward him.

"Espresso?" he asked.

"No thanks," she said, eyeing his sludge. She'd grab a cup of Dunkin' at the airport.

The pit of her stomach was quivering with excitement about this trip. For one, the clothes. Sure, they were all black and white and gray, but she'd never worn such a nice outfit as the black pants, black sweater and black boots she currently had on. She looked like a really cool assassin, she thought, or a French woman. Same vibe. Her bag was the only thing that wasn't new, but it was a Kate Spade backpack in emerald green, a gift from Addie a couple of Christmases ago, and it added a cheery splash of color.

She'd never been to San Francisco before. Hopefully, she'd have some time to walk around a little if Lorenzo didn't need her. Get some chocolate at Ghirardelli, maybe, or ride a cable car.

"Here's your boarding pass," Lorenzo said, texting it to her.

She looked at it. Seat 2B. "Is this in first class?" she asked.

"Yes."

"Cool." She'd never traveled first class before. According to Addison, first class meant a cleaner bathroom and a seat an inch or two bigger than in economy. Thrilling, the privileges of wealth.

Lorenzo sipped his espresso and stared out the window. He really was attractive, Winnie thought. She wondered if he had an arrangement with someone for sex (though if he did, it wasn't on his calendar). At the restaurant last night, a woman had been very obviously staring at him, which Winnie found unsubtle and also rude. They weren't together, but they could've been. Happily, Lorenzo ignored her, or just didn't see her. Winnie suspected the latter. He was not the type whose attention wandered, and last night, his attention had been on her.

I want you to look like the successful woman you are.

That sentence had been both a slight insult and also incredibly validating. She was getting used to that combination from Dr. Satan.

A car service picked them up at 6:30, and traffic was only on a scale of 8, 10 being a standstill. "We probably could've walked here faster," she observed.

Lorenzo didn't answer, eyes on his phone. "I'm sorry, I have to call the hospital," he said. And then, right before her eyes, he transformed from Lorenzo Santini into Dr. Satan.

"This is Dr. Lorenzo Santini. What is your name?" he asked, his tone sharp as a razor. "I've just read the chart for Mrs. Singh, *Nurse Hall*." Her name sounded like a curse. "How is it that you haven't managed to check my patient's vital signs in the past two hours? She was in surgery for five hours yesterday, *Nurse Hall*, and survived a complicated tumor removal in addition to having two feet of her small intestine removed. What if she's bleeding internally, *Nurse Hall*? Well, how would you know? The chart says her dressing was soaked. Do you want her to die of an infection because of your neglect, *Nurse Hall*? You don't. Well, that's very reassuring to hear. Are you a critical care nurse? You're a *floater*? Jesus Christ. If you're ever assigned to one of my patients again, you tell Verline I specifically said you were not to be involved in their care. Put her on right now. Yes, Verline the charge nurse, for God's sake."

Winnie met the driver's eyes in the rearview mirror. *Yikes*, she telegraphed. He lifted an eyebrow. Guess he drove for Lorenzo regularly.

"Verline, it's Lorenzo Santini. A floater? For one of *my* patients? I understand you're short-staffed, but...yes. Thank you. I appreciate that." He ended the call. "Incompetence," he muttered. "I hate incompetence."

"Yeah, that came through," Winnie said. "Will your patient be okay?"

"Yes. A very good nurse has been assigned to her, one who's cared for my patients before. They're not *all* standing around like idiots, scrolling on their phones when they should be working."

"The Dr. Satan thing is making sense."

He slid her a glance. "Don't forget you work for Dr. Satan."

"You're proud of that nickname, aren't you?"

He looked at her again, and maybe there was a hint of a smile in his eyes. She smiled back. If she worked for Dr. Satan, did that make her head demon or something? She could get behind that title...

"Here we are, Dr. Santini," the driver said, pulling up to the curb at their terminal. "I'll get your bags."

Inside was the usual airport chaos. Lorenzo headed right for the scanners that seemed right out of a cautionary sci-fi movie. "You'll have to go through regular security, so I'll meet you at our gate. Please apply for the facial recognition scan for the next time we have to travel."

"Okay," she said, watching as he walked away.

The security line would take a while, so Winnie used the time to text Robbie.

Guess where I am? Logan, that's where. Going to SF with Dr. Satan for a medical conference.

Wow, Winfrey. You sound wicked important.

I am. You should know that by now.

Bring me a souvenir.

I will.

I want a sea lion.

Done. Tell Rosie I said hi. Oh, and tell Mom and Dad where I am. And Grandpop.

> Let's wait to see how long it takes for them
> to notice you're gone. Like that time at the
> rest stop, remember?

She did remember. Not her parents' finest moment. Winnie had been eight or nine, and they'd been going to see Mom's parents in New Hampshire. When they stopped for a bathroom and snack break, Winnie had been the last one out of the bathroom. She went into the food court. No Smiths that she could see. She went outside. No Mom, no Dad, no siblings. The car was not where she remembered it. Long story short, they'd left without her. So Winnie sat down on the curb and waited. People walked past her, giving her odd looks. One woman bent down and asked if she was okay. She didn't answer, unsure if she was, unsure what to do. She decided she would wait half an hour (she'd gotten a watch for her birthday), and then call the police if her parents hadn't found her by then. The woman stayed, standing a few feet away.

Twenty minutes later, they were back: Mom full of apologies, Dad panicky, Robbie clutching himself with laughter, Lark sobbing, Addie irritated, Harlow comforting. As she got in the car, Winnie looked at the woman who'd stood there and gave her a small wave. She realized the woman had been standing guard, making sure she wasn't kidnapped. Winnie appreciated that.

The story became family legend—how the other four had been noisy enough and distracting enough that her parents hadn't noticed they'd left her behind.

She sent Robbie a middle finger emoji and finally got to the security check and went through. She stopped at Dunkin', got her coffee (extra cream) and headed for their gate. Plenty of time. The suitcase was more like a dance partner than something she had to drag, it was so smooth and easy to maneuver. She wove in and out of the crowd, her excitement rising with every step. She'd looked up the hotel last night—The Mark Hopkins. Her room was on the same floor as Lorenzo's suite and contained a king-size bed, huge tub for the bath she would definitely take, and a view of the Golden Gate Bridge. Wicked, wicked cool.

The new clothes were really nice, too. Ridiculously expensive, but she understood that she was supposed to convey a certain élan as his assistant. She'd played it cool in the shop yesterday, but her inner Julia-Roberts-from-Pretty-Woman was squealing (and she didn't even have to become a prostitute!) The clothes were the type she'd have chosen herself if she won Mega Millions—well made, great materials, classic but with a little bit of an edge—the black dress had an asymmetrical neckline, cutting down on the left side to expose her collarbone. The gray sweater had mother-of-pearl buttons up the back, and the white suit jacket had cool pleats in the back. The mix-and-match of black and white would give her a lot of options. She would keep her hair in its sleek ponytail, maybe a tidy bun. She'd also bought some lipstick at CVS, though she rarely wore makeup, but what the hell, right? Maybe she'd pick up some different earrings or a bracelet when she was out and about, if she got to leave the hotel, that was. She didn't know how medical conferences went.

There was her gate. She pulled the borrowed suitcase close and looked for Lorenzo. He didn't seem to be there yet. Maybe he'd gone to a lounge to wait for boarding, though it started in ten minutes. He was not the type to be late, though, so she wasn't worried. She wondered if he had dinner plans with his fellow surgeons, and if so, what she would do for the evening. She'd text Harlow, who'd been to

San Francisco a few times. Rosie, too, would know some good places.

Then she heard a familiar voice.

"Boarding group seven? Ugh. Why is it always seven, right? I should've paid for the upgrade. Once we're on, though, I'm sure we can find a way to make the time pass faster."

She could hear the smile in his voice. She turned, and there, about ten feet away, stood Chef Mitchell-Tanner Prescott-Johnson—talking to a beautiful woman in her twenties. She was beaming at him.

Another girlfriend? Already?

Then he saw her, did a double take, then turned back to the woman.

Ignoring her. Like she didn't even exist.

"Mitchell?" she said loudly. "Mitchell Prescott, is that you?" She closed the distance between them. "Or are you going by Tanner Johnson today? Or do you have a new name now? Anyway, how's your wife? And the kids? Everyone's good, I hope?"

"Winnie. Hello."

Winnie turned to the gorgeous young woman. "Just in case you're dating him, I was, too. He's married. Three kids, the oldest just turned five. He never mentioned them the whole six months we were together. You might want to dodge this bullet." She looked back at Mitchell-Tanner. "I'm so glad I made you use condoms, but I did get an STD panel just in case. I bet your poor wife has to get those all the time. I was clean, by the way."

"Is that true?" said the young woman. Mitchell-Tanner pulled a face. "Jesus, you're disgusting." She turned to Winnie. "Did his wife text you?"

"Worse. She blasted the whole thing at his son's birthday party."

"You didn't do a background check?"

"Believe me, I did. He uses a different name professionally. My bad."

"Well," said the woman, "I'm not dating him. But thank you. And, girl, next time, check out HesAPieceOfShit.com. It uses AI to scrape all the dating apps."

"Great tip. Thanks."

The woman turned sharply, her braids swinging, and took a few steps away, then pulled out her phone.

"Don't worry, Mitchell-Tanner. I'm sure you'll find another woman to lie to," Winnie said, her cheeks—and heart—hot with anger.

Mitchell looked at her, his face pitying. "Oh, Winnie. You're a grown woman. You knew what you were getting into."

"I didn't know, *Mitchell*, because you told me you were single. You lied for *months*."

"More like you were lying to yourself, babe. You literally brought nothing to the table other than easy access. Obviously, we weren't serious."

She sputtered. Not serious? He'd asked where she might want to take a honeymoon! "Your *wife* thought we were serious. The wife I didn't know about, just to drive that fact home."

"She and I have an understanding."

Winnie snorted. "Yeah, right. That was totally clear when she had her meltdown at *your child's* birthday party."

"Blakelee knows I have to flirt with patrons from time to time."

Winnie felt her blood pressure soar. There was a

buzzing in her ears. "You did more than flirt with me. We were together for six months! You said you loved me."

As soon as the words were out of her mouth, she regretted them.

"Oh, God, Winnie, really? Did you *really* think I meant it? Wait. I forgot you…how did you put it?… You'd only *shared yourself* with one other guy." He made air quotes around those words, words she'd wrestled with for half a day, trying to find a way to tell him she was inexperienced. "So maybe you *are* a bit stupid when it comes to men."

Then someone was standing next to her. Lorenzo. He was looking at Mitchell, expressionless, his blue eyes like Arctic ice. "Sir," he said, "if you would like to get to your destination without a black eye, I suggest you sit down and shut up." Then he looked at Winnie. "Everything all right?"

"Yep. Though I think a black eye would be a great look for you, you cheating asshole. I'd like to do the honors, though." Her heart felt huge and wrong in her chest, flopping and convulsing like…like a dying sea lion.

Then Lorenzo did something shocking. He took her hand. "Don't waste your energy on trash, darling. Let's go. They're boarding first class. After you."

With her head feeling oddly disconnected from her body, she went to the gate attendant, fumbled with her phone and flashed her boarding pass to the gate agent. "Welcome aboard, Miss Smith," he said, and Winnie walked down the jet bridge to the plane. "Right this way, Miss Smith," said the flight attendant. "Dr. Santini, welcome aboard." She had a window seat. She stood there, still feeling sick. The attendant put their bags in the overhead compartment, then asked if they'd like champagne or coffee.

"Champagne for both of us," Lorenzo said. Winnie got into her seat, buckled the belt, and stared out the window.

Mitchell-Tanner was on the same flight they were. He was going to San Francisco, alone, but she guessed he'd find someone to screw while he was there.

The memory of his searing words landed in her chest, and suddenly, her eyes were full of tears. She felt Lorenzo sit next to her. A second later, he pushed a glass of champagne into her hand. "Drink that." She did, in one gulp, wincing as the bubbles burned down her throat. He handed her his glass, and she took a smaller sip, unable to look at him.

People were coming onto the plane now, filing past them. "We're going to be deep in conversation when that man walks past," he said. "Here. Take a look at my presentation for tomorrow." He opened his laptop. "You'll get to see this before anyone else. Consider it a privilege of the job."

He tilted his head close to hers as he opened the Power-Point. *Handling Unexpected Complications During Level Five Abdominal Surgeries* read the first slide.

"Ah," she said. "I've been dying to learn about this."

He glanced at her and again, a remarkable thing happened. He smiled. "Prepare to learn," he said. "Let's take slide number four. Hepatopancreatobiliary surgery, or HPB for short, is almost always to remove metastatic or primary pancreatic tumors. Some HPBs can be minimally invasive, but for the presentation, I'm focusing on more aggressive interventions, such as a Whipple procedure."

"Of course," Winnie said.

His voice was low and gentle as he explained the basics of this type of surgery. The medical terminology, something she'd heard from her dad and Lark all her life, was oddly musical.   Laparoscopic.   Cholecystectomy.   Biliary. Duodenum.

His shoulder was warm against hers as he spoke, and she appreciated that he assumed she could follow along. He was not condescending, but he sensed what terms a layperson might not understand and explained in a concise, logical way. He must be a good teacher, she thought as she finished his champagne.

"The background of your slides is a little dull," she said. "There are dozens you can choose. If you want, I can do that for you. Maybe bullet-point some of the terms and use some visuals."

He looked at her, a little surprised. "Well. Don't change the text or anything."

"No, I wouldn't. I can just make it a little more appealing. Friendlier, easier to look at."

"That would be...agreeable, I suppose," he said.

"I'll do it as soon as we get to the hotel."

"Thank you." He held her gaze, and she noticed that his eyes weren't icy at all. They were just blue. A very nice shade of blue, actually. Clear, medium blue. She should probably think of something more descriptive than that, but it really wasn't her way. "You look very nice, by the way," he added.

"You get the credit for that," she said.

"I think your parents get the credit for that." Another smile. Was he flirting with her? No. But...no. She'd bet her pinky finger Lorenzo Santini, M.D., Ph.D., had never flirted in his life. "All clear," he said.

"Sorry?"

"Your former person is on his way to steerage. You're safe."

"Steerage?" she said. "Don't call it that, Lorenzo." But

she was smiling. Hey, she'd sat back there in the rear of the plane. He wasn't wrong.

And then, maybe because of the champagne, she was laughing harder, giggling, and then her eyes were wet again, and the laughs stopped and maybe some crying was taking place.

"He didn't deserve you," Lorenzo said quietly, handing her a handkerchief. He had a handkerchief. Of course he did. Then he turned back to his laptop, closed the Power-Point, and opened a different document and began typing.

It occurred to her as she closed her eyes that what Dr. Satan had done—from the second he appeared at the gate to showing her his presentation to ignoring her right now—was among the kindest things anyone had ever done for her.

ELEVEN

LORENZO

When Winnie had woken up from her nap on the flight, he'd gone over the conference program, noting which speakers he might want to hear and briefly explaining the topics. Damian Hughes was giving a talk on how to handle unexpected findings during an elective surgery. A little league topic.

"Like if you're putting in breast implants and find a tumor?" Winnie asked.

"Yes. Like that. But that rarely happens because imaging is so accurate these days."

"Maybe in some less-funded places, you'd be more likely to be surprised," she suggested.

She had a point. But knowing Damian, the talk would be sophomoric—teratomas, no doubt, along with the accompanying pictures for effect. That was one way of keeping an audience's attention. The other was to have a deep understanding of the topic.

"What else would be an unexpected finding? Like a tooth or hair in a tumor?"

The exact definition of teratoma. "Yes. There have also

been times when parasites are discovered, or a sponge from a previous surgery. Abscesses, necrosis, chocolate cysts."

"Gross," she said, a hint of admiration in her voice.

"At any rate, I won't be going to that one. It's pure showmanship. Zero value to someone like me."

"Mm-hm." She looked back to normal now, thank God. "Which doctors do you want to meet up with?" she asked, looking back at her laptop screen.

ONCE THEY CHECKED in at the hotel, he gave her the spare key card for his room if she needed to access it, then went up to his room. He'd stayed in this suite before, and it was elegant and comfortable. He texted Winnie:

Is your room satisfactory?

Very.

He appreciated her brevity and lack of emojis, something his sisters and mother seemed unable to live without. Then, with a sigh, Lorenzo left his room. The conference didn't start until tomorrow, but he would go to the iconic Top of the Mark, look out the windows at the view, and let his colleagues approach and chat him up. He hated that. Not the conversing, just the glad-handing and small talk. So unnecessary.

He texted Winnie again.

I will be socializing in the bar with colleagues. You have the rest of the day off.

He hit send, then, a second later, added:

Enjoy

WHEN HE CAME BACK to his suite later that evening, he was hungry—he hated eating at professional events—irritable, thirsty (must each glass of water be seventy-five percent ice?) and tired. It took a moment for him to notice his room looked different from earlier in the day.

Ah. A cut-glass bowl of oranges sat in the center of the round table in the living room area of the suite. A bottle of Brennevin and two glasses were set out on the coffee table. On another table was a basket that contained protein bars—Jacob, the kind he liked best. In addition to the orchids that had already been in the suite, there were two glass vases containing huge, fluffy dahlias in a very pleasing shade of pale peach. Also, a printed itinerary of the next three days, complete with times, locations and speakers of the talks he'd indicated. His own presentation would be at 1:30 tomorrow and was in boldface. She had entered "potential downtime" in the gaps during the day.

He liked hard copy. Holding a sheaf of papers put people off more effectively than holding a phone.

There was also a note, printed in a slightly different font from the itinerary.

Dear Lorenzo,

I sent your blue and gray suits to be pressed, as well as your shirts. They'll be brought up to your room before 8:00 a.m. tomorrow. There is mineral water in the fridge and a bottle of Brennevin if you decide to have a drink. There are also some protein bars (all natural and organic)

*on the counter. I put a pack of travel-size candles on
your night table in case you like that sort of thing.
Supposed to help you destress and sleep (dubious, but
worth a shot). I am nearly done jazzing up the Power-
Point and will send that to you later tonight so you can
review it.*

*I will be awake and ready at 7 a.m. in case you need
anything. I hope you sleep well.*

Winnie

*P.S. The flowers are to thank you for being so kind at the
airport. They also cheer the place up.*

Well. That was…that was very thoughtful. Should he thank her? No. She was thanking him. Also, he remembered her saying flowers cheered up his house in Chatham. The little joke was not lost on him.

He wondered what she was doing. If she'd had dinner. If it would be appropriate for him to ask her to have dinner, since he'd given her the time off.

Lorenzo knew he was perceived as an arrogant prick (rightfully so, he could acknowledge). Work was sacred to him, requiring complete and utter focus and only the best team members. Sure, he tore residents new orifices on a regular basis. Yes, he shredded nurses who weren't attentive enough. He had to. Because although he wasn't warm and fuzzy, he had a 95.7% success rate of not just patient survival but of a meaningful, functional recovery and acceptable quality of life. This included the emergency and high-risk patients who were so often his patients. So 95.7%…that was just a number he was deeply proud of. He would not change anything. His grandmother had understood that being at such a high level meant sacrificing other parts of his life. "I doni che Dio ci ha dato non si devono sprecare, Renzo," she would say. *The gifts from God must not be wasted.*

Which, summed up, meant Lorenzo did not have much in the way of friends or a social life. He ran six miles every day (had done so just after unpacking today), but running wasn't a hobby. It was a duty. He read, but only nonfiction medical works. He had colleagues, a mentor or two, some surgical residents and a few post-op nurses whose intelligence and work ethic he respected.

His college roommate from Harvard, Obasi, kept in touch, but he did humanitarian work all over the world. Every other year or so, Obasi would return to Massachusetts, drop him a text, and they'd have a very amiable afternoon together. They'd both been pre-med and had become rowing partners in school, and when they got together, they'd rent a double scull and go out on the Charles if the weather was nice. That was friendship, Lorenzo thought. When Obasi had gotten married, Lorenzo had gone to Nigeria for the wedding, even. Alone.

He also had Dante, of course. Henry, Sofia's husband, was okay. A solid husband, which was what mattered.

His stomach growled. His watch said seven o'clock, though jet lag made it seem later.

He texted his assistant.

Have you had dinner?

Within seconds, her answer came.

I have not. Would you like to meet, or should I arrange something for you?

He hesitated, then asked,

> Where are you?

Three dots told him she was answering. The dots disappeared. He hated when that happened. Phones could be so annoying, telling a person just enough to irritate. Then the dots reappeared. Good.

> I'm in Pacific Heights and just walked past an Italian restaurant that smells like heaven. Sharing my location with you now. Do you need an Uber?

The location came through. He checked Google Maps.

> I'll walk. See you in 22 minutes.

The map said it would take him 33 minutes to walk, but Lorenzo was tall, fit and walked so fast that residents had to run to keep up with him. Also, he was eager to eat, especially with someone who did not irritate him.

Florio's was warm, dimly lit and, as Winnie had said, smelled like heaven. Or at least, like his grandmother's kitchen.

She was already there, sitting at the bar with a martini. She must've gone shopping during her off-time because she was wearing jeans and a red sweater with a wide neckline. She smiled when she saw him and moved her bag from the stool next to her. "No Brennevin, alas," she said. "I already checked."

"That's fine. By the way, thank you for all the...details. The oranges, et cetera. The itinerary. They are appreciated."

"Those flowers are sick, aren't they?"

"Did you buy those yourself?"

"Yes."

"Bill me."

"No, Lorenzo. They were a thank-you gesture. I can afford a dozen dahlias."

"All right, then."

"Hey, man," said the young, tattooed bartender. "What can I get you tonight?"

"Just water," he said. Then he added, to offset the stress of these conferences, "And whatever she's having."

"You got it. Miss, you ready for a refill?"

"All set," she said. "One and done."

"Smart lady." The bartender smiled at her—*smile*-smiled, Lorenzo thought. And why wouldn't he? Winnie Smith was an attractive woman. He glanced at her to assess her reaction. She didn't seem to be affected, even though (objectively speaking) the bartender was very good-looking in that hipster way. Earrings, beard, hair gel.

"How long are you in the city?" the bartender asked Winnie, barely looking at Lorenzo as he made his cocktail. A gin martini, from the look of it.

"Just a couple of days," Winnie said.

"If you need any recommendations on what to see, say the word," he said, and Lorenzo felt a flicker of annoyance.

"It's a work trip, but thanks," Winnie said.

Lorenzo accepted his drink from the far-too-handsome bartender. "Thank you," he said, dismissing him. He turned to Winnie. "How was your sightseeing?"

"Great," she said. "What a beautiful city! I love all the Victorian houses. And the gardens! There are calla lilies everywhere. Makes me want to move here."

The bartender started to comment, and Lorenzo shifted to block him a little more. This was not dinner for three. It was for two. "Have you ever lived anywhere other than

Cape Cod?" he asked. The bartender got the hint and drifted to the other end of the counter.

Winnie shook her head. "No. I'm not very well-traveled, unfortunately."

"No semester abroad?"

"No. I only went to community college for a couple of semesters. I didn't really know what I wanted to do, so I stopped going. Seemed like a waste of money, honestly."

"Most kids in college are absolutely wasting money. Or their parents' money, at least."

"Right? Harlow did undergrad *and* law school, and now she runs a bookstore. At least she had scholarships." Her face flickered. "But it was still time well spent. I mean, she had my nephew in that time period. And met Rosie."

"Mm." Seven years of higher education to run a bookstore? It *was* a good thing she'd gone on scholarship, or her debt would be staggering. He sipped his drink. He rarely ordered a cocktail, but he supposed the practice wouldn't hurt. Most doctors he knew drank at least once in a while, given the state of healthcare these days—being threatened and heckled by ignorant mobs during the pandemic who then came mewling back for medical advice when they got sick. Having insurance companies dictate which tests were necessary, which medications were needed, how long a patient should stay in the hospital. The high cost of medical school and medical malpractice insurance. There was reason to drink. It made him glad to be a surgeon, not the poor beleaguered general practitioners or ER doctors like Lark.

"Would you guys like a table, or would you like to stay right here?" asked the bartender, his eyes on Winnie. "I mean, I have to say I'd miss you if you left."

"What do you think, Satan? Stay here? It's pretty cozy."

He had been about to ask for a table, but he paused when she called him Satan. It was growing on him. "Whatever the lady wants," he said, wondering if he sounded stupid.

"We'll stay," she said to the bartender. The bartender handed them dinner menus, winked at Winnie—inappropriate—and left again.

"Did you ever live abroad?" Winnie asked.

"I did a six-month fellowship in Denmark, and two stints with Doctors Without Borders. One in Haiti about five years ago, one in Palestine six months ago."

"Wow. How long were those?"

"Because I'm a surgeon, the time periods were shorter. Nine weeks in Haiti, seven in Gaza."

She nodded, looking at him, toying with the toothpick that had held the olives in her martini glass. "Good for you, Lorenzo. I bet you did some great work there. They must've peed themselves when you showed up."

He smiled a little. "Hopefully not."

"Well, as you like to tell me, you are the shit."

"I'm quite sure I've never used those words."

"Semantics. Let's order. If I order spaghetti and meatballs, will you think I'm a peasant? Or, rather, will that reinforce your view of me as a peasant?"

He started to answer, to tell her that her services were quite helpful, he did not regard her as a peasant at all when he realized she was making a joke. "Get whatever you want."

"Only if you do, too. And I'm not talking about which meal has the highest nutrient count or whatever. Get something you really want. Something that makes your mouth water. I mean, if you can stand to bend the rules for one night, Dr. Santini. You're already doing so well by ordering a martini."

She smiled at him, and suddenly, his brain locked. Not because of anything...romantic. Just because Winnie Smith's smile made her face something he wanted to study. To memorize. She had gone from a somewhat plain-faced woman to utterly...intriguing. Which came as quite a surprise, to say the least.

Chi studia un bel sorriso, dimentica la strada di casa, Noni used to say. *He who studies a beautiful smile forgets the way home.* A warning. Winnie seemed to be waiting.

What was the question? Ah. Dinner. "I'll have the lasagna, in that case. I'll have to run twelve miles tomorrow to pay for it."

"Or not. You could get a salad, too, which would erase all that delicious cheese and meat."

"It wouldn't," he said.

"No! Really? Then I've been lied to my whole life," she said, smiling again.

Maybe it was the warm and cozy restaurant, or the rain that had started outside, or the gin in his admittedly excellent dirty martini. Maybe it was because the bartender had finally gotten busy enough to leave them alone. Maybe because Winnie Smith was being friendly and cheerful, but Lorenzo was having...a very nice time. A *relaxed* time in which he was smiling occasionally and asking an attractive woman questions about her life and listening to the answers, mostly interested to hear what she had to say.

And luckily, he told himself, there was no chemistry between them, which would've made things complicated and difficult. No, he hadn't touched her. Unless you counted on the airplane, but he thought he could be excused for that. She'd been in crisis. He had intervened.

"How did you get involved with that idiot from the airport?" he asked as they shared an unplanned order of focaccia with an olive tapenade.

"I ate in his restaurant. He was the chef, came out, chatted me up, asked for my number." Emotion flickered under her skin, but her expression didn't change. "I didn't know he was married. His wife obviously found out. She hired me to throw her five-year-old a birthday party, and outed me as a scarlet woman. My brother even got me a great sweater with the letter A embroidered on it."

That didn't seem very supportive. Then again, Lorenzo himself had done some assholery on the cheating front, but only with his brother's best interest at heart, and long ago at that. "She outed you?"

"She announced that I seduced her poor hardworking husband, because you know..." She indicated her torso and face. "Scarlett Johannsen right here, right?" He didn't know who that was, so didn't answer. "Anyway, I tried to explain, she didn't believe me—who would? And then I got...a little outspoken at a restaurant and basically finished digging my grave, at least in the event-planning world."

In his normal life, back before he had a personal assistant who made him feel looked after and at home, he would not have enjoyed this conversation about messy personal moments. "What does being a little outspoken mean?" he asked

She shook her head, rolled her eyes and said, "Four glasses of wine, a microphone and a packed house. I told the crowd that A) I knew who slept around, so no stones in glass houses, right? And B) I thought their little parties were mostly stupid."

"Did you? I'm impressed. They *are* stupid. My sister had a gender reveal party for both her kids, and I sat there thinking, 'What if you miscarry, Sofia?' and also, 'Is this really necessary?'"

"Exactly! It's such bad luck!"

"Fai festa troppo presto, e il diavolo infila la coda."

She pulled back a little to look at him. "Go ahead, show-off. Translate, please."

"Celebrate too early and the devil slides in his tail." He lifted his glass in a toast.

"Oh, I like that one." She took a bite of her food. "Out of professional curiosity, I have to know. How did they do the reveal?"

He smiled. "For William, who came first, they had a picnic and asked Henry's mother to bring her falcon."

"Did you say falcon?" She was already smiling.

"I did. And at the appropriate moment, the falcon swooped in, hit a huge balloon with its talons, and poof. Blue powder all over the food. We had to order out."

She threw back her head and laughed. "Whoops! Well, points for creativity. I've never heard of that one before. How about for Lucy? By the way, Lark is crazy about her. She's Lucy's godmother."

"Yes, I'm aware, as I'm Lucy's godfather." The instant irritation that always flared when someone told Lorenzo a fact he already knew was absent this time. "Anyway, they learned their lesson about exploding powder. They just bought a stork pinata and beat the thing to death until pink candy rained out. It was extremely violent. Not child-appropriate in the least."

"Hopefully therapy will clear William's mind of the memories. Tell me more about your family. I'm on the fringe, but I know Dante, of course. Your sisters seem wicked nice, and your parents, too."

"Yes, they're all wicked nice."

"But…"

"But nothing. They're nice people."

"That's not how people usually talk about their families, Lorenzo."

He gave her a look. "It's how I talk about mine."

"Here, I'll demonstrate. My parents are irritatingly happy with each other and like to show the world that they're winning at marriage. Lots of public displays of affection, lots of snuggling and flirting. As their child, I'm glad for them and just wish I saw less of it. No one likes to see their parents making out, you know? And also, it's…well, it's a lot to live up to."

"Mm." His own parents were less demonstrative, but very much a unit. He'd never thought about their marriage much, to be honest. Assumed it was solid based on the evidence presented.

"My oldest sister is the best," Winnie went on. "She had a baby in college and placed him for adoption, but they reunited and he's awesome. Lark and Addie are complete opposites in every way but DNA. No one likes Nicole, Addie's wife, except Addie, so I guess that's what really matters. Addie seems shallow and irritating, but she'd also kill for you. Lark…well, you know Lark. She's an angel sent from heaven."

"She cries far too often. She definitely cried at the gender reveals. She'd gotten very attached to that stork."

Winnie grinned. "And finally, there's my brother, Robbie, who's a jerk, who falls into the best things without lifting a finger, and just when you think he's a complete idiot, does something great for you. And we can't forget my grandfather, who's perfect in every way. So. That's my family. You try again."

His good mood seeped away. Also, he should not finish

the lasagna, no matter how fantastic it was. "My family is fine. I told you I didn't grow up in the same house as my siblings."

"That school for gifted kids sounded very cool."

It hadn't been *cool*. It had been a privilege, yes, but also utterly terrifying to a seven-year-old boy. Thank God he'd had Noni to help him manage that first year.

"So what does the Santini family do together?"

"We eat."

"Yes, I would imagine." She waited for more, her interesting eyes patient and interested.

The food was pleasantly heavy in his stomach, and the wine—because at some point they appeared to have ordered some—was softening the sharp edges of his mind. "I don't feel as...connected to them as I think I should be," he said. "It was always the five of them, and then me. I didn't know the inside jokes. I wasn't there for the daily routine. I became an oddity within the family. I lived with my grandmother, who was a very strong woman, very supportive, but it was..."

"Lonely."

He nearly flinched at hearing it put so bluntly. "Yes."

"Did you like the school?"

"Also yes." He started to speak, then pulled the words back. He'd been lucky to go to St. George's. Lucky to have had a grandmother who understood how fast his brain metabolized information, who encouraged him to be the best, who pushed his teachers to challenge him. She had marked each of his accomplishments with a combination of pride and certainty. Of course he was first in his class. Of course he scored perfectly on all standardized tests. Of course he graduated early from both high school and college. He missed her—that one person in his life who had seen him so clearly, put him on a path where he could reach his potential.

But whenever he'd gone home and seen Sofia, Dante and then baby Isabella, he'd felt like a stranger. Even his parents didn't know him the way his grandmother had.

"The school was really great for a kid like me. But it also caused a split, I suppose. I grew up like an only child, living at my grandmother's house. I don't know my family all that well, to be honest, even now."

He took a sip of wine—Winnie had chosen it, and the velvety texture was pleasant, as was the lingering taste of blackberries and smoke.

"How about Dante? You were best man at his wedding. You must be close."

Lorenzo shrugged. "We had a...falling out a few years ago, but we're past that now." He still felt a flash of shame when he thought about it.

"Over what?" she asked.

He hesitated. "He was dating a vapid woman. She made a pass at me. I, uh, accepted."

"Oh, my God, Lorenzo!"

"Keep your voice down. I only did it to demonstrate her lack of...character."

"You slept with her?"

He looked at the floor. "Yes. Just that once."

"Wow."

"Yes. And before you lecture me, I know it was wrong, and I apologized. Dante let it go. He was head over heels for her. I thought he'd need indisputable proof that she didn't actually love him."

Winnie ran a hand over her head, smoothing her pony-tail. "I bet there was a better way to show him that."

"In hindsight, absolutely. In the moment, it seemed like a clear-cut and efficient way to prove the point."

"Wow," she said. "Wow."

Like most men who'd made a mistake, it had taken Lorenzo a long time to acknowledge his. But when he had finally gone to his brother and apologized, and said how much he regretted hurting him, Dante had just looked at him for a long moment, then hugged him. "I know you thought you were doing a favor, Lorenzo. I dodged a bullet with her, and in some weird way, I have you to thank for it. We can let it go now, okay?"

Definitely okay.

"So now you guys get together and toss a football?" Winnie asked.

"Not exactly. My hands are insured."

"Really? That's wicked cool. I mean, a shame you can't play ball, but so cool your hands are insured." She gave a half-nod. "You know, I wasn't sent to a school for smart kids, that's for sure. But I get it, that feeling of being on the outside."

"Really? You all seem very close."

"Sort of, yes. I think I just got lost in the shuffle. Two of my sisters were valedictorian, Harlow resurrected our grandmother's bookstore, Lark's a doctor, everyone goes nuts over identical twins, Robbie's the only boy *and* the baby. Addie kind of sucks up all the air in the room with her perfect life and perfect children—by the way, they're demons, never let them in your home. And then there's me. Competent, but otherwise unremarkable in just about every way."

It was his turn to pull back and look at her. "That's not a word I would associate with you."

Her cheeks flushed, and her eyes were that fascinating

blend of green and gray and gold, maybe a hint of blue now. Not unremarkable in the least.

"Mm. Well, that's nice to hear, and thank you. But it's not exactly the stuff of dreams, you know?"

"Being good at your job should be the stuff of dreams. You've made my life more organized and efficient, and therefore more pleasant. I appreciate that."

"I'm glad you feel that way."

He wanted to tell her it wasn't just organization skills and efficiency. It was her thoughtfulness. Those scented candles, even if they were somewhat ridiculous, the flowers, the bowl of oranges. Every detail she'd been taking care of since he'd hired her had left him free to fill that space up with something more important, or just...just to breathe, really. That first night in Chatham, when they sat on the deck, for example. He needed to do that more. This very dinner, which had given him a reason to walk in the famed fog of San Francisco rather than stay in and order room service and review his notes. Right now, he was doing something he never did—having dinner with an interesting, funny, competent and rather pretty woman. One who hadn't flirted back with the bartender—she was too elegant for that. She asked questions without being nosy, listened to his answers and wasn't the least bit intimidated by him. In his eyes, she was quite...special.

But he had no idea how to say that, and the moment passed. It was better that way.

"Would you like to walk back to the hotel?" he asked.

"I think I'll take an Uber," she said. "The wine is making me sleepy. It's also raining pretty hard."

Normally, he would've said fine and walked himself, alone, briskly, to facilitate digestion and clear his head. But that would be rude, and while being rude was his trademark, he did not want to be rude to Winnie Smith. "I'll see you to your door, in that case."

They didn't talk on the ride back, which was brief. At the hotel, he followed her to the bank of elevators, nodding to a few doctors he knew. They got off on their floor. "Which room is yours?" he asked.

"Right down here," she said, pointing to the end of the hall. He walked her down, waited till she opened the door. "Thank you for a lovely dinner, Lorenzo," she said.

"Thank *you*," he said, meaning it. "You're excellent company."

She smiled a little, then said, "Sleep well," and closed her door.

Usually, Lorenzo did sleep well. That night, he did not, and for the life of him, he could not understand why.

TWELVE

WINNIE

Winnie woke up feeling fantastic. No fuzziness, despite her cocktail and wine the night before, no jet lag, no urge to stay in bed. She pulled up Yoga with Adriene on her laptop for half an hour of yoga—her legs ached pleasantly from walking up and down the hills of San Francisco. Adriene had a session for that, of course, and Winnie stretched and bent and balanced.

The part of yoga she disliked was the meditation. She'd never been able to *empty her mind* as instructed. As she lay there in corpse pose, a thought circled that she wasn't sure she wanted to push away.

Dinner with Lorenzo last night had felt like a date. A really good date.

Not that she'd had much experience with that sort of thing. Before Mitchell, she'd tried the automatic go-to for single people—online dating. Bumble had directed her to a carpenter in Provincetown (gay, looking for a woman to create a threesome for him and his apparently bisexual husband). Hard pass. The next guy had had social anxiety to the point where he actually slid under the table to avoid talking to a server. She'd gotten him up, walked him to his car and recommended therapy, texted him a day or so later to see if he was okay and learned that he'd moved to Arizona to live with his sister. The next man only wanted to text, not meet, which Winnie thought was ridiculous.

For her business, she'd actually run a couple of singles nights, but as the person in charge, she just watched. Had some guy approached to chat her up, she would've been game, but no one had. No one ever did that kind of thing anymore. Not to her, at least.

And then there had been Mitchell-Tanner. In hindsight, it was so clear—he'd asked her to the restaurant at closing only, or have her come to his place to cook for her. But he'd never taken her anywhere. He'd also love-bombed her...flower arrangements, special desserts, five-course dinners made at his condo. Dozens of texts every day telling her he missed her, couldn't stop thinking about her, had never felt this way before about anyone. *You're so beautiful. I dreamed about you last night. Is it wrong that I'm picturing our wedding?* He'd bought her pearl earrings (which she later returned and donated the money to a homeless shelter). Silk pajamas and sexy underwear. He told her she was beautiful, sexy, addictive, and she fell for it. She felt like a different woman, the Winnie loved by this fictional man.

But last night with Lorenzo, she'd been completely herself...just the best version. Maybe because it *wasn't* a date, though it was their second dinner together in a week. He was simply her boss, and he hated schmoozing, and they both simply needed to eat. There was no pull between them, as there had been with Mitchell-Tanner. Granted, Satan's looks were growing on her. Initially, she'd thought of him as bland as, oh, one of those suit models in GQ, chiseled but unremarkable. But when he granted her the upward tug of a smile, she felt a little like she'd just won a prize. His hand, as he'd helped her off her stool at the end of dinner, had been warm and firm.

There was also the fact that she liked talking to him. He was interesting and a little quirky. She liked his stiff, almost old-fashioned way of speaking. But she'd had actual fun last night. She'd been his PA for seven weeks now, and while most of her work had been without him there, she was getting to know him. His love of precision and order, which doubtlessly was part of his surgical talent, was something she could relate to. Her little house in Wellfleet was always immaculate, everything in its place, tidy and comforting.

There was more to Lorenzo than a condescending asshole with God complex, that was for sure. Last night, she'd had the sudden thought that it wasn't just his sense of superiority that kept him from other people...it was that he was socially awkward, not intending to put people off, but unaware of how to put people at ease. He'd essentially been put on a path at the age of seven with one goal and one goal only—to be the best. He didn't know *how* to converse, relax, or spend time with people for the pleasure of their company. He'd been trained not to, in fact.

An idea struck her, and she leaped off the hotel-provided yoga mat and flipped open her laptop. It took all of ninety seconds. She saved the file, sent it to Lorenzo via email, then texted him.

> Just sent you an updated version of your PowerPoint. Make sure you use this one.

There was no answer. She took a shower, got dressed in her fabulous new clothes—the black suit with the blindingly white shirt made her feel like someone to be feared and avoided, which she could definitely lean into. She added the red lipstick she'd bought at CVS, and yes, she was *absolutely* a force to be reckoned with.

No answer to her text. Maybe he was in the gym or had gone for one of his punishing runs. She checked his location, and nope, he was here in the hotel, and from the look of it, still in his room.

> Did you have breakfast already?

If not, she could grab him something from the buffet. Still no answer.

It was nearly eight o'clock, and the workshops started at 8:30. He wanted to attend one about crush traumas (she kind of wanted to sit in on that one, gruesome though it would be). Then he had a panel at ten, with his own presentation at 1:30, right after lunch.

She gathered up her laptop and slid it in her backpack, which held a printed itinerary, three bottles of mineral water, a tin of tea bags she'd assembled—peppermint, licorice and ginger, in case all this talking would bother his throat, and a protein bar. She also had twenty business cards, which she'd nabbed from his study in Boston in case he forgot them.

Chief of Special Surgeries,
Mass General Brigham Hospital
Moseley Professor of Surgery,
Harvard University Medical School

She'd looked up those titles and found out that Lorenzo was the youngest person ever to hold those titles. Dr. Satan was pretty badass indeed.

That being said, Satan had yet to respond to her text,

and his blue dot was not moving. She walked down the hall and knocked. There was no answer. Texted him.

> Open your door, you're late.

No response. She knocked harder. "Lorenzo? Are you in there?" She knocked again.

"Jesus! Coming!" He opened the door, and her eyes widened. He was wearing boxers, an open hotel bathrobe, and his hair was sticking up in odd places.

"Are you sick?" she asked.

"Yes. I have a horrible headache, my stomach feels like something died in there, and the light hurts my eyes. You'll have to cancel my talks."

She smiled. "Lorenzo. You're hungover. Come on, let's get you human again."

"I'm not hungover."

"Oh, yes, you are."

"This must be meningeal irritation or a migraine."

"Or a martini and two glasses of red wine for someone who rarely drinks alcohol."

He closed his eyes and sighed. "I guess that tracks. Can you close the curtains? The light is like a knife in my head."

She obliged, then dug around in her bag and took out a bottle of Excedrin and got a bottle of Gatorade from the fridge. "Take two, drink all the Gatorade and get in the shower. I'll run down to the breakfast buffet and get you something to eat."

"I never want to eat again." He tossed back the aspirin and chugged the Gatorade, grimacing.

She went to the first floor, where a gorgeous breakfast buffet spread out, and loaded up a tray with an everything bagel, a bowl of yogurt, two bananas, and a hefty plate of scrambled eggs and bacon. Added a large glass of orange juice and two mugs of coffee, then went back to his suite, letting herself in with the keycard he'd given her.

"Breakfast has arrived," she said, setting the tray on the coffee table.

He came into the room wearing pants and holding his shirt. All righty, then. Lorenzo was, um, very fit. His muscles rippled under his skin as he pulled it on, and Winnie watched, a little...hypnotized. Fascinated. She obviously knew his workout and running schedule. She just hadn't pictured it manifesting so...nicely.

"Sorry, what?" she said, forcing her eyes away.

"I don't eat that kind of breakfast."

"Trust me. I have experience in treating hangovers."

"Is someone in your family an alcoholic?"

Rosie was, sober for more than two years now, but that was none of his business. "A former roommate," she said, which was also true.

He ate the yogurt and bananas, drank the orange juice, and took one bite of the bagel. "Do you want anything?" he asked belatedly.

"No, thanks. I'm fine. I'll get something downstairs. By the way, the crush injury workshop you wanted to see is in the Stanford Room. That's on the mezzanine level." She handed him his very gorgeous, buttery leather bag, and they walked down the hall to the elevator. When they arrived on the ground floor, he looked at his watch.

"Thank you for waking me up," he said.

"Do you feel any better?"

"I do. Thank you."

She smiled. "You're welcome. I'll check in with you before your panel. It's in the Six Continents room, also on the mezzanine."

"Very good. Thank you." Off he went, once again the consummate professional.

A FEW HOURS LATER, Winnie sneaked into Lorenzo's panel, which was on diversity, equity, and inclusion in surgical programs. The room was packed, so she stood at the back.

Lorenzo was one of four doctors—a Southeast Asian female who looked to be around fifty; a young Black woman, who was maybe thirty-five; then, oddly, two white males—Lorenzo and an older man with white hair and a white beard. Weird that half the panel was white men, given the subject.

Lorenzo looked bored, staring at the table rather than the audience as the older man spoke. Winnie hoped his hangover was better (but it *was* pretty adorable that he'd had one and hadn't been able to diagnose it himself).

A glance at the program showed Winnie that Lorenzo had more titles after his name than anyone else, though Dr. Jackson (the other white guy) was professor emeritus at Baylor. Dr. Kharal was the vice chair of the surgical department in Cleveland, and Dr. Bahrani-Jones, the youngest panel member, was simply listed as surgeon at a hospital in California. She had the floor now.

"A more diverse group of surgeons builds trust in marginalized communities," she said. "A survey done last year said that Black and Hispanic people were less likely to follow through on recommendations for surgery, and that the race of the surgeon—88% white—was definitely a factor."

"So you're saying minorities won't come to me because

I'm white?" Dr. Jackson said sarcastically. "Come on now. That's overly simplistic, even for you, Dr...." He paused and looked at the card that bore her name. "Dr. Bayron-Jones, is it?"

"And right there is an example of racial and gender bias, with a microaggression thrown in for good measure," Dr. Bahrani-Jones said. "My name is not hard to pronounce. As for my comment being overly simplistic, *even for me*...We've never met before, Dr. Jackson. You have no idea of my intellect, yet you've already implied that I'm not very smart, based on my gender and skin color. You're also trying to negate the facts of this study because I'm the one who presented them."

"Being politically correct is not good for science," Dr. Jackson said. "This is *medicine*. We can't hire people just because it looks good." An uncomfortable murmur went through the audience.

Lorenzo sighed but didn't look up from his staring contest with the table.

"I would also like to address your statement and way of thinking, Dr. Jackson," Dr. Kharal said. "Thinking like that is part of the problem. You assume my colleague here, and perhaps I as well, had an advantage because of gender and race. In fact, we have had to work twice as hard as our white male colleagues."

"Oh, please. Don't try to beat *that* dead horse. Surgeons have to be the best of the best. You ladies got your feathers ruffled. And don't try to play the racist card. I've got Black friends." Dr. Bahrani-Jones rolled her eyes. "In surgery, we need the finest candidates, like Dr. Santini here. We can't be hiring just anyone to make us look *woke*." He used finger-quotes.

"Being woke is better than being asleep at the wheel," Dr. Bahrani-Jones said.

"Dr. Santini, you haven't said much," said the moderator. "Care to comment?"

"Yes," Lorenzo said, finally looking up. He leaned forward to his microphone and looked at the crowd. For a second, he didn't say anything, and the crowd grew silent. Winnie bet it was a well-used trick of his, staring people down before he spoke. "Dr. *Jackson* is part of a dying breed of outdated physicians who believe that equity and inclusion weakens quality." Winnie stood up straighter. His tone dripped with the quiet, lethal venom he'd used on the nurse who hadn't checked his patient the other day. He was about to live up to his nickname, and a ripple of electricity went through the room.

"Dr. *Jackson's* assumption is a rejection to every fact we have available. Dr. *Jackson's* bias is an example of how archaic thinking creates an institutional environment of hostility and exclusion," Lorenzo went on. "*His* definition of quality depends on the exclusion of certain types of people. He is confusing his own insecurity with a decline in quality where no such decline exists." He turned to face the older man. "Dr. Jackson, your words have revealed you to be what most of us in this room already know—you are ignorant of facts, dismiss data and, if we are to believe you, are racist and misogynistic as well. In other words, Tom, your ass is showing."

Spontaneous applause broke out, with a few hoots and whistles.

"No," Lorenzo said sharply, death-staring at the audience—mostly white men, Winnie noted. "You didn't applaud my female colleagues when they said the same thing in more polite language. Listen to *them*. They have lived experience. They are each gifted surgeons who have faced prejudice and a lack of opportunity. I'm a white male with every privilege of education, financial security and opportunity. Neither Dr. Jackson nor I should even be on this panel. Where is Dr. Ruiz? Dr. Hussein? Dr. Hughes? Dr. Kagame?" He stood up. "Dr. Jackson, you should probably leave, since your paleolithic mind has been closed for decades. As for me, I'm going to sit in the audience with my mouth shut so I can listen and learn."

Someone started to clap, then abruptly stopped when Lorenzo cast them a look so sharp it could've drawn blood. He left the dais, and Dr. Kharal leaned forward. "Thank you, Dr. Santini," she said smoothly. "I believe the next topic on our agenda is the lack of mentorship programs for women and people of color in residency programs. Dr. Bahrani-Jones, would you care to discuss this?"

Heads were careful not to turn as Lorenzo took a seat in the back third of the room. Winnie pulled out her phone and texted him.

> Well said, Dr. Satan.

A second later, he texted back—a devil emoji. That was it.

She looked at the back of his head, where every hair was in place, and smiled.

THIRTEEN

The thing about doing the right thing, morally speaking, was that it never brought the right results.

Lorenzo knew his takedown of the idiotic Tom Jackson would ruffle feathers. He didn't care about that. What he hated was the attention it brought *him*. Granted, Dr. Bahrani-Jones and Dr. Kharal were surrounded by colleagues after the talk. But so was he, for a few congratulatory slaps on the back and "good for you" type of comments. Dr. Damian Hughes, the obsequious ass-kisser, approached. "Perfectly stated, Lorenzo," he boomed. "And thank you for the shout-out. Nice to know you're an ally. I've been creating an outreach program to Stanford Medical, trying to encourage other people of color to shadow me for a day or so in surgery, and—"

"Good," Lorenzo said. "Excellent. Please excuse me." He ran the same kind of program, actually, and had written an article for the *New England Journal of Medicine* about the need for more, but he hated this kind of virtue signaling. He also knew that as a leader in the field, he had a duty to participate in the conversation. Carol van Thynge, a colleague from his residency at Yale, raised her glass at him from the bar, and he gave a nod as he felt his neck stiffening. God, he'd do anything right now to have his hands on a hemorrhaging abdominal aorta. Better than all these people looking at him.

Where was Winnie? He'd love to see someone who wasn't a surgeon.

"Time for your presentation," she said, suddenly at his side. He startled a little. "You good?" she asked.

"It's very crowded in here," he said, glancing around the lobby. A bar had been set up on the terrace, a beautiful, glassed-in space, and many of the doctors were not shy about day drinking.

"Yes, well, conferences will do that. Let's head over and I'll double-check the connection for your PowerPoint, okay?"

"Lorenzo! It's about time someone told that old fart to go to hell!" came a voice. Miguel Rivera, chief of surgery at Houston Methodist.

"Yes," Lorenzo said. "Well."

"And who is this?" Miguel asked.

"My assistant, Winnie Smith."

"Hello," said Winnie, her face neutral. He really liked that about her. No gushing, no ass-kissing, no trying to make an impression.

"Lovely to meet you, Winnie, and it's about time someone helped this man manage his time. I don't think he ever sleeps!"

"Good to see you, Miguel," Lorenzo said.

"Listen, I wanted to talk to you about establishing a sort of exchange program between our hospitals. Do you have ten minutes?"

"Sure," he said. No time to run through his notes or ensure his PowerPoint was working. "Winnie, can you—"

"Already on it," she said, and walked off.

———

THE ROOM WAS STANDING room only for his lecture. He'd known it would be. He was, after all, perhaps the world's leading expert on this topic. At least, the nation's leading expert. But definitely in the top five worldwide. He wasn't bragging. It was simply true. He'd graduated from high school at sixteen, college at nineteen, flew through medical school, getting his Ph.D. and M.D. the same year (thanks, Harvard). He then skipped to the head of the line for surgical residency, and by the end of his first year, had already proved himself (again) as intellectually gifted and remarkably adept with a scalpel. He'd been called rockstar, ninja, wizard, ace, cowboy, hotshot, and superstar. There were surgeons, and there were gods, and Lorenzo was one, and he knew it.

Which actually meant life outside of a hospital was strange and uncomfortable for the most part. Not many people understood his world. They could not appreciate the delicacy, the hand-eye coordination, fine motor control, the 3-D mental mapping of anatomy, the ability to interpret imaging in a nanosecond, the critical thinking, the grace under pressure, the focus, the almost psychic sense of what was about to happen.

But this crowd knew. Here, he could teach. Here, he didn't have to flay a lazy resident. This crowd had already earned their chops, or were in the process of it. Dr. Khalal was in the front row, and Dr. Bahrani-Jones gave him a nod as she sat down. Damian Hughes was also in the front row, the better to be seen. His assistant was at his side, pressing a bottle of water into his hand, whispering into his ear, head bowed. Lorenzo was glad Winnie didn't do that.

After the moderator gave his lengthy bio, Lorenzo approached the microphone stand. The introductory page of his presentation was already on the screen, and he realized he hadn't looked at the updated version, given the humiliating hangover that caused him to oversleep. Winnie *had* jazzed it up, as she'd put it in her email. The font was a basic but elegant serif, the colors navy and white, with statistics in yellow. She had resized the photos and framed them so they were easier to see.

Lorenzo never ad-libbed or went off course. He knew what he had to say, and it was all spelled out right there on his laptop. "Good afternoon," he said and got to work.

As he clicked through, discussing abscesses and ischemia, fistulas and vascular injury, he fell into the language of his chosen field. The audience was scribbling notes, tapping into their laptops, murmuring. A few hands were raised, but Lorenzo only took questions at the end as a rule.

"And with that, mesenteric perfusion is preserved," he said, finishing up that slide. "Next, of course, is this rare but not unheard-of complication." He frowned, not recognizing the words as what he'd written. He clicked, then, not understanding what he was seeing on his screen, turned to look at the big screen. A wave of laughter rolled through the room.

It was a cartoon, likely from the *New Yorker* or something like it, showing an OR, a surgical team standing over a patient. The caption showed the doctor saying, *"Everyone be quiet, and the nurse will call my phone."*

He looked up, and the laughter increased. Why? *He* was not smiling. He hadn't even put that in there. He—

Winnie stood in the back, near the exit, and she was looking at him. She pointed to her mouth and smiled, wordlessly instructing him to do the same.

A mild panic wrapped in coldness gripped his chest. A *cartoon?* Humor? In *his* presentation? It was so unprofessional. The laughter was confusing, so out of context during one of his lectures. Winnie pointed more vigorously to her bared teeth.

Di' qualcosa, idiota, he heard his grandmother's voice saying. Not that she ever called him idiot, but yes, he should speak.

"Just one more reason to leave your phones in your lockers," he said, his voice neutral. Another laugh rippled through the crowd. "Moving on to metabolic failure."

FOURTEEN

WINNIE

Winnie was pumped. Talk about the perfect icebreaker for Dr. Satan, especially after he'd burned Dr. Jackson so spectacularly. The cartoon had done its job—made Lorenzo seem like he didn't take himself too seriously every second of every day.

Since he didn't have anything else on his schedule for the rest of the day and had responded "no" when she texted to see if he'd need anything from her this afternoon, Winnie decided to see a little more of San Francisco. She let Lorenzo know, then changed into the jeans she'd bought yesterday and a sweater. She found a bike at one of those city-wide rental stands and set off for Golden Gate Park. The botanical gardens were beautiful, and she stopped often to wander down a path. The bridge sprawled across the bay, the sky so blue against the soaring, orange beauty. She got a hot dog, then decided to ride across the bridge, the cars whizzing past, pedestrians stopping for selfies so often she nearly hit them (and occasionally regretted missing them).

On the other side, she rode up to the Marin Headlands

and sat, the sun warm. It was beautiful, so…ethereal, almost. In another life, Winnie could picture herself living here. Or maybe even in this life. Her gig with Lorenzo was temporary, after all. She'd never imagined leaving the Cape, but that was probably because she'd never really left the Cape. In fact, this trip was the furthest she'd ever been from home.

Note to self: travel more. With what Lorenzo was paying her, maybe she could sock away some money for a trip.

She saw a low cloud coming in off the sea—the legendary fog! It rolled and tumbled, and the blue sky was abruptly blotted out, the temperature dropping ten degrees. Carefully, she rode back to the bridge and across, the fog so thick now she couldn't see the northbound traffic. She went to Ghirardelli Square, opted against chocolate and bought an ice cream sundae instead, as well as a sweatshirt, since she was now officially cold.

She texted some pictures to the family chat, then called Grandpop, who was delighted to hear from her, and Mom and Dad, too, because she was feeling beneficent and maybe wanted to let them know how cool she, the unremarkable daughter, was. *On a business trip to San Fran, yes. Very busy and important.* Not that they'd ever voiced any disappointment in her, but it was still fun to show off a little bit.

Nothing from Lorenzo. For some reason, a small quiver of unease shot through her. But no, it was good that he didn't need anything. He'd smashed it today, in both his panel discussion and his solo presentation. And he had colleagues to meet and other talks to attend and all that. Probably a lunch or dinner. Tomorrow was more of the same, though Lorenzo had no speaking obligations, and they'd head home the day after that.

The fog rolled back out, and the sun set gently, the sky

pale gold before fading to violet. She pulled off her new sweatshirt, tucked it in the bike's basket, and rode down Lombard Street, as one does in the City by the Bay. All around her, lights went on, and it was the most extraordinary feeling—she, Winnie Smith, comfortably wandering through a strange city.

Life was full of surprises. And life could unfold in all sorts of unfamiliar ways. Like so many people her age, she had never assumed she'd find a solid job, stay there for a couple of decades, earn enough to buy a house and go on vacations. Getting by would be a great accomplishment. But leaning into the unexpected, taking a swerve off a path...for whatever reason, she had never thought of herself as one of those people.

But here she was, with her highly respected boss in a city she'd only seen in movies, wandering through the unfamiliar streets and reveling in the newness of it all.

She had never thought of herself as someone who would be dressed in a starkly beautiful outfit, wearing red lipstick. Someone who might bike through one of the most beautiful cities in the world, let alone someone who was staying at an iconic hotel in a room that had a view of the famous bridge. Someone who'd had dinner at a cute Italian restaurant, who was good at her job...not just good. Maybe great, she thought, thinking of Lorenzo's hangover this morning, the laughter over the cartoon during his presentation.

Eventually, she returned her bike to a BayWheels station. Grace Cathedral was closed, but the outdoor labyrinth was open to the public, and she walked it, hoping she was being contemplative enough. Then she headed back to the hotel. As she walked down California Street, a young man flew past on a skateboard. "Hey, mamí," he said.

"You're beautiful, you know that?" He made a kissing noise as he whizzed past her. He was maybe sixteen years old.

"Thank you, papí," she called, grinning. She actually *felt* rather beautiful today.

Well. It was seven-thirty, and she wasn't exactly hungry, but she wanted to wear that little black dress. Up to her room she went, took a quick shower, and got dressed.

Damn. The dress was killer. Maybe that kid on the skateboard was right. With her red lipstick and lovely high-heeled shoes (high for her, at least), she felt...confident. Pleased. Pulled together and sophisticated. Having three gorgeous older sisters, she'd always felt that "clean" was about as much as she could pull off.

Tonight, she felt...well...different.

She pulled her hair back into its neat, tight ponytail, looked at herself for another second in the mirror. Yep. Butter on bacon, as Grandpop would say. Then she slid her credit card and room key into her pocket (because the dress had pockets!) and went down to the lobby. No one was there, and the terrace room that had served as the bar was now mostly empty.

"Looking for the other surgeons?" asked a staff member.

"I guess so, yes," she said.

"They're upstairs."

"What's upstairs?"

The man smiled. "The Top of the Mark. One of the most famous bars in America. Best views of the city in all of San Francisco."

"Okay, then. Thank you."

"Enjoy your evening, Doctor," the man said.

She paused. "I'm just an assistant."

"You don't look 'just' anything to me," he said with a wink.

He was flirting. First the bartender last night, then the kid on the skateboard, and now him. "Thanks," she said, smiling, then headed back to the elevators.

The Top of the Mark was all that. Posh, crowded, glamorous. San Francisco glittered out the windows, the triangular Trans Am building looking close enough to touch. The Golden Gate Bridge looked so romantic from here—and she'd just been on it! There was Grace Cathedral, Alcatraz, the Pacific.

The bar was packed with the sort-of familiar faces she'd seen over the past two days. She recognized Dr. Bahrani-Jones at a table by the window. The moderator from Lorenzo's lecture. A white-haired woman who'd asked her where the California room was. She did not see Lorenzo.

"Please, miss, take my seat," said an older man at the curving, beautiful bar. "I'm about to head out."

"Thank you," Winnie said, sliding onto the stool. She ordered a gin and tonic and just sat there happily, in this alternate reality where she was complimented and men gave her their seats and she belonged in this fancy-ass hotel. It wasn't the most beautiful bar she'd ever seen—the Red Inn in Provincetown held that honor, with waves breaking against the windows during high tide in the winter. But still, it was simply gorgeous. She sipped her drink and just listened to the music and chatter around her.

"Thank God for that cartoon," someone said. "Kept us all from going to sleep. Honestly, he is so full of himself. I get it, he's talented, but the guy is as dry and dull as dust."

Heat flooded Winnie's cheeks. It was clear who the subject of the conversation was.

"Now, Damian," said his companion. *Dammy-AHN.* "He's intense, that's all. And brilliant. I recorded his entire talk."

"Oh, I know, I know," Damian said. "But then there's the way he bullies his residents. Dr. Satan, my ass. If I saw him lay into someone the way rumor says he does, I'd probably punch him in the face."

"Sure, Dam. Sure you would."

"Listen, I'd let him work on my own mother. But I'd also shoot myself in the head if I had to talk to him alone for an hour."

"I wouldn't," said the other person. "I'd practically interrogate him. Did you know when he was a resident, he saved a man who'd sliced his carotid? Stuck his hand in the man's neck and pinched it off, held it all the way to surgery, then sewed it back together in under a minute."

"Yeah, yeah, we all have that one story we milk for all it's worth. Did I ever tell you about the woman I saved after she fell onto an iron spike? She was climbing over a gate. Not sober, let me tell you. Singing at the top of her lungs, according to her friends, and then *foop!* She's essentially eviscerated herself, pinned like a butterfly."

Winnie glanced over her shoulder and saw the speaker was a good-looking Black man in a gray suit with a pink shirt, clearly amused with his own well-told story, laughing loud and hard. She knew his type. People with those carrying voices and great stories who let every person in the room know *they* were the main attraction, the light around which the moths should flutter.

Also, Lorenzo was not dry or dull. And yeah, maybe he was Dr. Satan, but he was also fucking brilliant. He just existed on a plane not many people could reach, that was all.

She turned back and took another sip of her drink, then jumped as Lorenzo himself sat down next to her. "Winnie," he said.

"Hi! How was the rest of your day?"

"Do not ever tamper with one of my presentations again," he said, his voice low. "That was humiliating."

"What?" She sat up straighter, then lowered her voice. "It wasn't humiliating, Lorenzo. It was funny, and it let the audience know you have a sense of humor."

"I *don't* have a sense of humor," he said. "I *am*, however, greatly skilled at handling complications during very difficult surgeries. *That* was the subject of my talk, and yet seventeen people thus far have commented on your ridiculous cartoon."

"Yeah, okay, but it showed you were human. Also, you do have a sense of humor. It's just not blatant. It won't hurt your reputation as a surgeon, and it just might help your reputation as a speaker."

"My reputation as a speaker is unimpeachable. Or it was until today."

She wondered what he'd say if she told him what Dr. Pink Shirt had just said.

"People laughed," she said. "They paid attention."

"They *always* pay attention."

"Yes, but think of it as a comedic break during a very serious lecture. A chance for them to take a breath for a second."

"Winnie, I know my audience better than you do."

"Great talk today, Lorenzo!" came a voice. "Loved the OR humor, too." He turned to Winnie with a smile and offered his hand. "Hello! John Granger, Linda Loma Medical Center. And you are?"

"She's my personal assistant," Lorenzo said, barely registering the man.

"Winnie Smith," she said, shaking his hand. She recognized his name from Lorenzo's schedule next week. "Nice to meet you."

"Same here! Great to see you, Lorenzo. We have that conference call coming up, don't we?"

Lorenzo glanced at Winnie, and she gave a slight nod. "Correct," he said.

"Excellent! Well, have a great night, and safe travels back East."

"Nice to meet you," Winnie said, then turned back to Lorenzo. "See? Told you. The cartoon was great. Now order a drink."

"No, I will not. Winnie, I want to be clear. I did not appreciate your addition to my presentation."

"Yes, that comes through loud and clear. Sorry. It will never happen again, even though you're missing a chance to connect with people."

"I don't *need* to connect with people," he growled. "It's not part of my job. My *job* is to save lives in situations where most physicians would fail, and I do that quite well." His eyes were shooting spiky icicles.

"Yes, you're the second coming. I'm well aware, since you remind me every two hours." She took a sip of her drink.

"Sir, what can I get you?" the bartender asked Lorenzo.

"San Pellegrino, no ice," he growled.

"Please and thank you," Winnie said to the bartender. "He's mad at me, not you."

The guy winked and got Lorenzo his water.

"Here's the thing, Lorenzo," Winnie said, keeping her voice quiet. "You're right. Your reputation is unimpeachable. But you don't fool me. You're a good guy. You just don't want anyone to know that."

He rolled his eyes. "What makes you think I'm a good

guy, Winnie? And also, why would that matter as long as I do my job well?"

"Because you're more than your job." She kept her voice low, matching his. "You're a good guy because you look after your family. Granted, it's by writing checks, but maybe that's your love language."

"What in God's name is a love language? Never mind. I don't want to know."

"You tipped the bartender fifty percent last night. You left the hotel cleaning crew a hundred dollars yesterday and today. You kicked that wrinkled old doctor's ass in that DEI presentation and then made sure everyone in that room listened to the other doctors. You think that went unnoticed?"

He grunted. Finished his San Pellegrino, which was mostly ice.

"And you were very nice when I saw Mitchell the other day," she added.

"Who's Mitchell?"

"Oh, save it. You know full well who he is. You love your siblings, even if you don't feel a hundred percent comfortable around them, and you take good care of your family. I'd venture to say that you even love children, even if they terrify you. I mean, your expression in some of those photos is nothing short of dumbstruck with love."

"I have never been dumbstruck by anything, and children do not terrify me. You should probably make that cocktail your last."

"It's my first."

"Did you have anything to eat today?"

"Yes. Eggs Benedict for breakfast, a hot dog, then a huge ice cream sundae at Ghirardelli's."

"You'll be dead of a heart attack by fifty if you keep that up."

"At least I'll die happy and well fed."

He almost smiled, just a shifting of the muscles of his face, a glint in his blue eyes, and she felt it in her stomach, a warm, curling squeeze.

Hey, now. What was that?

"Back to the subject at hand, Satan," she said briskly. "It wouldn't hurt you to let your guard down a little."

"I think it could hurt me quite a lot," he said, and he looked at her for a long minute, and in his clear blue eyes, she saw something she didn't exactly expect.

He was lonely. He was brilliant, and sought after and busier than most people on earth, and he was lonely.

A bellow of laughter came from Dr. Pink Shirt's table—Dammy-ahn—and Winnie glanced at them again. There he was, leaning toward another doctor as he glanced at Lorenzo. He pulled a face, laughed, and slapped the other person's back and said something to his companion. And maybe it was because she was fourth of five children, but Winnie excelled at eavesdropping, and she heard what he said.

"Such a pretentious asshole."

Nope.

Winnie hopped off the stool. "Excuse me," she said, taking a step closer to Dr. Pink Shirt and his buddies. "I overheard what you just said about Dr. Santini, and I couldn't help but disagree. He is *not* dry and dull as dust, and if he was, why do you trail after him like a lost puppy hoping he'll pat you on the head? Also, he's not pretentious because he doesn't *have* to pretend. He's a genius, and if you're too dumb to realize that, I sure as hell wouldn't trust *you* with a scalpel."

And then, in the silence that felt suddenly very obvious, she suddenly felt mortified. Behind her, she could *feel* Lorenzo's censure, simmering like lava about to erupt. How humiliating—his assistant, who hadn't even graduated from college, defending him. He was going to fire her for sure.

"Well. Thank you for your input, uh...Miss...person," Damian said. "Would you care to join us?"

"No!" she said. "Absolutely not." She turned to the bartender. "Charge my drink to my room, okay? 1503, last name Smith. Give yourself a twenty-dollar tip."

She didn't look at Lorenzo, felt the unexpected sting of tears behind her eyes. Her face was burning. It took a thousand steps to reach the exit, and she was terrified she'd turn her ankle in the unfamiliar shoes. So much for feeling glam earlier. She felt like an idiot right now. Finally, she was next to the elevators, jabbing the down button repeatedly.

"What is it about you and making a scene in bars?" Lorenzo asked, and she jumped, not realizing he'd followed her. "This isn't trivia night at the Ice House."

"How do you know about the Ice House?" she asked.

"Dante told me just after I hired you. You also told me yourself, just last night."

"Oh. Right."

The doors slid open, and it seemed like a hundred people poured out, leaving the elevator empty for the two of them. They stepped in, and the doors closed.

"I certainly don't need you defending me," Lorenzo said. "Dr. Hughes is a very good surgeon. He is not 'dumb,' as you said."

"He called you a pretentious asshole!"

"So?"

"So he was disrespecting you!"

"And?"

"And I didn't like it!" she exclaimed. "Because, Lorenzo, you're rare, okay? Even in this hotel, with all these surgeons from all over the country, you stand out. They all wish they had what you have. They all admire you. You have the brains, the skill, the integrity. And if the only way one of them can feel good about himself is to try to take you down, well, fuck him. And if me telling him off somehow hurts your beloved reputation, sue me."

He didn't sue her. He kissed her instead.

Okay, he did more than kiss her.

He pressed her against the elevator wall, cradled her head in his hands, and stunned her by pressing his lips against hers. It was so shocking that for a second, Winnie wasn't sure it was actually happening. But yes, he was kissing her, and then she appeared to be kissing him back, gripping his arms, then sliding her hands up along his shoulders. His mouth was warm and, um...yes, it was...yep. They were kissing. And it was...

Incredible.

Her organs seemed to be melting, and heat throbbed between her legs. Her mouth was doing things against his, and a low sound came from her throat.

Lorenzo was lean and warm and hard with muscle, and one arm slid around her waist. She felt dizzy with shock and lust and possibly with gin. She deepened the kiss without thinking, and he responded by pulling her harder against him. The bell dinged, and without moving his mouth from hers, Lorenzo simply picked her up and carried her into the hallway, her legs dangling against his, still kissing her.

Then he set her down in front of a door—his or hers, she didn't know—and slid his knee between her legs and lowered his mouth to her neck. If she hadn't been pressed against the door, she would've slid to the floor. His hand slid up her ribcage and skimmed the side of her breast while his other hand tugged at her ponytail, exposing more of her throat to his mouth.

She had never been so turned on in her life.

"Is this all right?" he muttered against her collarbone.

"God, yes." She tugged his shirt out of his pants. Lorenzo fumbled in his pocket, and she heard the click of the keycard reader. Then the door was open, and they were inside his suite, and his hands were cupping her ass, and all she wanted was out of these clothes.

"Wait, wait, wait," he said, his breath coming hard. "Are you...are you consenting to this? To sex? With me?"

She almost laughed. "Yes. Want me to write it down?"

"It would take too long," he said, and his mouth was on hers again, his tongue sliding against hers. She gripped his hair and welded herself against him. Then he picked her up and carried her into the bedroom and dumped her on the vast white bed and tugged off his shirt, the muscles sliding under his smooth skin.

Had he always been so beautiful? Had she actually been neutral about his looks before? With his hair tousled and his cheeks flushed, his blue eyes intent on her, she thought he was the most gorgeous man alive. She knelt and wrapped her arms around his neck, kissing him again, and felt his hands go to the zipper of her dress.

"Um...condoms," he said.

"Right. In the drawer. The hotel stocks them."

"Very thoughtful." He opened the drawer, fumbled around and pulled out the "intimacy kit," which Winnie knew, from having explored the one in her room, contained massage oil, a candle, condoms and some chocolate. Very thoughtful indeed.

Then he sat on the bed, looked at her for a long moment, and ran his hand along her hair. Then he unzipped her dress, sliding it off like a caress. "Beautiful," he whispered, and that was it. She was undone.

Then he pushed her back against the mattress, his weight utterly perfect on top of her.

ALL OF THAT had made sense last night. Now, not so much. Not at all, in fact.

She blamed the cocktail on a semi-empty stomach.

In fact, all of last night had been ill-advised. She'd told off a *surgeon* at a *surgeons' conference* in front of other *surgeons*. She, who knew nothing about medicine.

Then she'd shagged her boss. Quite possibly the most esteemed surgeon in the United States, a man who lived a life of wealth and huge responsibility. A man who overpaid her to pick up his dry cleaning and reorganize his cabinets, and water his plants.

A man who was her sister's brother-in-law, a man she'd have to see at future family gatherings. They would share a niece or nephew if (when) Dante and Lark had kids.

With each thought, another muscle in her body stiffened. Winnie was nothing if not pragmatic. She had an excellent job with Lorenzo. Sleeping with him was going to screw that up. He was not built for a relationship of any kind, and she was still on the rebound, probably. And even if she wasn't, there was a power dynamic issue here. Or something. What if she fell in love with him? God! She wasn't about to do that again. Look what had happened with Mitchell-Tanner. That sure hadn't made her life better, all that...devastation.

Winnie stared out the window, trying to be invisible. It was her superpower, after all, but she was half of the people in the bed, so... Could she slip out and dash down to her own room without him knowing? She'd feel better if she was less naked.

She moved a fraction of an inch, only to have Lorenzo bolt upright next to her. She froze for a second, then turned to look at him. He did not look thrilled to see her either. A beat passed, and then they spoke at the same time.

"This was a mistake."

She sagged with relief. Oh, thank God. They were on the same page. "Yes," she said. "But you know, uh, very... um, nice. Let's just never speak about it again, okay?"

"Agreed." He ran his hand through his tousled hair. "And yes. Very...nice."

Another long second passed as they didn't make eye contact. She glanced at him. He looked ten years younger, being naked and all. A tingle started between her legs. Lorenzo shifted a bit. *Get out, Windsor, before you do another thing you'll regret.*

"Okay!" she said. "Close your eyes, I'm getting out of bed."

He obeyed, and she got out, yanked on her clothes, ran her hands through her hair, and stepped into her shoes. "You have the organ transplant lecture at nine, a meeting with Dr. Connors at eleven and said you wanted to hear the lunch speaker. You've got time for a run at two o'clock, then the innovation award thing tonight."

"Yes."

"Anything you need from me?"

"No."

"Okay. I'll, um, just...I'll be around. Text me if you need anything."

"I will."

"Okay, great." With that, she left his room, forced herself to walk calmly yet briskly down the hall, and fished the key that was still in her dress pocket.

In the safety of her room, Winnie looked at herself in the bathroom mirror. Pink cheeks, messy hair, rosy lips. Definitely like a woman recently and well shagged.

She turned on the shower and adjusted the water to cold.

SIXTEEN

LORENZO

Thank God he was back in Boston, where he was more than happy to immerse himself in people's cavities, so to speak.

The last day of the conference had been uneventful. Nevertheless, a low current of electricity hummed in his bone marrow, uncomfortable and energizing at the same time. He avoided Winnie until the car service picked them up to bring them to the airport. On the flight, they both were very immersed in their laptops and had taken great care not to have an arm brush an arm.

"Do you need me here in Boston?" she'd asked as they got back to his apartment.

"I don't think so," he said. "But if you'd prefer to stay here and drive down to the Cape tomorrow..."

"I think I'll head back. I miss my family."

"Yes. Okay. I'll be in touch." He started to say something else...sorry, or thanks, or something. "Drive safely," was the best he could do.

"Talk soon." He watched as she walked to her car, put the suitcase in the back (he should've done that for her), then drove off. She waved. He waved back.

Do not sleep with your assistant. For the love of God, how had he made such a mistake?

Spontaneity was not something he ever indulged in. Honestly, he wasn't sure how it had happened. They'd been standing in the elevator, and then without knowing he'd made the decision to move, he had her against the wall, his mouth on hers. She could've kneed him in the groin, slapped his face, filed a lawsuit, or simply pushed him away and said, "No way, Lorenzo."

Instead, she'd kissed him back.

God, what a mistake. He remembered Lark saying he shouldn't hire someone he couldn't fire. Now he'd slept with her. She'd be stupid if she didn't sue him.

Her hair had slid through his fingers like water, and her skin smelled like honey. She was strong and soft and (God forgive him) limber, and he—

"Stop thinking about it, idiot," he said out loud. Unfortunately, he was in the hospital elevator, and a resident thought he was speaking to her.

"Sorry, Dr. Santini," she'd whispered. Later, he'd heard her say to a nurse, "It was like he *knew* I wanted to drop out." So now he was psychic as well as terrifying.

In the hospital, he was in a familiar, comfortable zone, the OR running like a Ferrari under his command. He resumed his exacting demands on his residents, though it didn't feel as automatic as usual. Almost like he had to work at putting the fear of God into them. Or fear of him, rather.

But it *was* necessary. Things went wrong when you were up to your elbows in someone's abdomen. Keeping calm as blood spurted and dripped and the smell of a ruptured bowel cut through your mask and the words of the surgical nurse and anesthesiologist were coming fast and furious and you had to absorb everything and make a decision in nano-seconds...*that* was what he taught.

Once his residents got past a certain stage, Lorenzo *did* lean into the mentoring aspect of teaching. But first, one had to *fare pulizia*, as his grandmother would have said. Clean out. *Chi è forte resiste, chi è debole cade.* The strong survive, the weak fall. Take Inez Cabrera, whom he'd be appointing chief resident soon. He'd called her out on an incorrect answer two years before. "The patient is alert and oriented, intermittent generalized pain, constipation for three days, stable vital signs. Her CT shows a closed-loop bowel obstruction. What course of action would you take, Dr. Cabrera?"

Her answer had been observation, no food, IV hydration.

Wrong.

"Did you miss the words *closed-loop*, Dr. Cabrera? Her symptoms are likely to intensify rapidly. Would you like to *observe* her blood pressure crash and fever spike? Shall we *observe* her bowel dying, Dr. Cabrera? Shall we observe the patient herself *die*, Dr. Cabrera?"

"No, Dr. Santini, and thank you for correcting me. I won't get it wrong again."

She had returned his gaze calmly. No crying, blushing or stammering, no making excuses or cursing him under her breath.

"Prep for surgery, Dr. Cabrera. You'll be assisting me." In the OR, she had asked intelligent questions, stood out of the way when appropriate, and adjusted her technique as instructed. And look at her now.

The Dr. Satan approach worked. Forged in the fires of hell, one of his residents had said. Damn right.

Outside of the hospital, he tried (and failed) to avoid thoughts of Winnie. He was unutterably grateful she agreed that it had been a mistake. A mistake that had felt really, really good. That honeyed skin under his mouth, the warm, soft weight of her breast in his hand, the soft, sweet noise she made when he—

Mistake! It had been a mistake. Period. Luckily, it had happened with the world's most pragmatic woman.

NINE DAYS after they'd returned from San Francisco, Lorenzo texted Winnie to say he'd be coming to Chatham for the weekend and asked if they could have a meeting when he arrived.

> If you're firing me, just say so now.

> I'm not firing you. Why would you think that?

> You haven't communicated with me since we landed.

> Because I didn't need anything other than what you've been doing.

He hesitated, then added,

> Are you quitting?

> No.

Oh, thank God.

Good. I'll be there around 7, depending on traffic.

See you tomorrow, then. The fridge will be stocked per usual. Text me anything else you might need before then.

A second later, she texted him a picture of his open refrigerator, another of his freezer. It had all the items he usually wanted. He knew also there would be clean linens and towels and the house would be immaculate. Flowers in vases here and there, sometimes in an unexpected place, like his bedside table or on the bathroom vanity.

It was a little hard to remember how he'd operated before Winnie worked for him.

He thought of her smile, how she laughed at something he'd said over that dinner in the little Italian restaurant, even of the lasagna that had been so damn good. He thought of the devil emoji he'd sent. The first time he'd ever sent an emoji, come to think of it. Her silky hair, sliding from her ponytail like a whisper.

Good thing he had a liver transplant in half an hour, so his mind went to easier subjects.

WHEN HE PULLED into his driveway at 7:14 the following night, it was already dark. He could hear the gentle rush of the waves and inhaled the salty air. The house glowed with light, and an assortment of pumpkins and gourds was artfully arranged on the granite entryway, spilling down the two steps. A wreath made of dried flowers, vines, eucalyptus branches, and seed pods hung on the door. Very tasteful, he thought, though he didn't usually acknowledge the holidays, other than having a Christmas tree (Douglas fir, white lights only, no decorations).

He paused, considered knocking, reminded himself that it was his house, and went inside. There was a cluster of white candles on the coffee table (in hurricane vases, he was glad to see). The dining room table held three small flower arrangements in a row, brilliant shades of red, orange, and yellow. A larger arrangement of the same flowers sat on the marble counter. The bowl that usually held lemons now held red and gold apples.

He opened the freezer. There was a martini glass, chilling. He was tempted to smile.

"Hi."

He turned, and there she was, wearing jeans and a green sweater, hair in her usual ponytail falling neatly down her back.

"Hello. Would you like a drink?"

"I'm actually planning to go home tonight, so no, thank you."

He poured himself some Brennevin, then gestured to the living room. "Please have a seat."

She did. So did he.

He had missed her, he realized.

"The flower arrangements are very seasonal," he said, feeling an unusual sense of awkwardness. "Which florist did you use?"

"Oh, I do them myself. Trader Joe's sells flowers."

"I see." He took a sip of his drink. "Winnie. I would really like to keep you as my assistant."

Something in her face relaxed. "Good. I like the work."

"And about the...San Francisco..."

"About the fact that we slept together," she prompted.

"Yes. That. I apologize. It was inappropriate."

"It's okay. It was consensual. And it's done, so…"

"Yes."

"Do you want me to sign something? A statement or waiver or whatever?"

"Do you think you should?"

She tilted her head. "You mean, will I sue you for sexual harassment or something like that? No. I won't. But if it would make you more comfortable, I'll sign whatever it is. I basically want to put it behind us."

That was…well, he wasn't quite sure how to take that sentiment. "Good. Fine. I'll take your word for it. No papers needed."

"Great."

"The house looks very nice, by the way." Homey. Welcoming. It hadn't felt that way, before he had her. It had been dark and cold, and it took several hours to warm up if the furnace had been turned down.

"Glad you like it."

"The gourds are unusual."

"There are ten of them. One for each member of your family."

He mentally counted. His parents, himself, siblings, siblings-in-law, niece, nephew. She was correct. "That was very thoughtful."

She smiled. "Do you need my services this weekend?"

"I don't." He didn't think he did. She would know better than he would at this point, he'd turned so much over to him.

"Great. I printed out letters from patients and their families, by the way. They're on your desk in the study."

"Thank you."

"Oh, one more thing," she said. "You know your neighbor, Joyce? In Boston?"

Lorenzo was unaware of a person named Joyce in his building.

"She lives in 3B? Anyway, she and I met when I first started working for you. She asked if I might have some time to help her organize her place. Would that be all right with you?"

"What you do in your own time is up to you." He paused. "I won't need you in Houston next week. It's only one night." Was that rude? Had he just hurt her feelings?

"Okay. I'll double-check your flight and hotel and all that." She paused, and he waited, hoping she'd say something profound. Something that would help him understand the chaos of feelings he was having right now. "By the way, do you know who owns that sweet dog? The golden retriever who romps on the beach most days?"

"No. I've actually only seen her with you."

"Huh. It was pretty cold out the other day, and she was all alone for a while. I—ah, never mind. Have a nice night, Lorenzo. See you tomorrow."

Her feelings did not seem hurt in the least. "Very good. Wait. Tomorrow?"

"My brother's bachelor party."

"Oh." His heart fell with a nearly audible thud.

She laughed. "I feel the same way, but he's my brother. The bus will pick you up around six." A bus? "Dinner first, then whatever else Austin has planned. The words mini-golf were mentioned, so maybe it won't be all bad. See you then." With that, she gave him a quick smile, grabbed her backpack, and left. He heard the garage door open, then close, saw the flash of her headlights cross his living room wall, and let the quiet settle around him.

A night in his lovely home. Alone. And while that had

always been something he looked forward to—cherished, even—it felt a little empty. Hollow.

Maybe he should get a dog.

***

WHY HAD he agreed to this particular circle of hell? Lorenzo asked himself as the bus lurched around a corner. There were so many people on this bus—himself, Winnie, Dante, the elderly Mr. Smith, Grady, who was married to the bookstore sister, Robbie himself, and the bride's father, Victor Wolfe, an entertainment attorney. Then there were half a dozen man-children who whooped and yelled and chugged. Victor Wolfe had become their god for the night, as he told stories of celebrities behaving badly and was paying for the entire night.

It hadn't started out awful...dinner at the Chatham Cut, an excellent steakhouse. He sat between Winnie's grandfather and Rosie's father. Robert Smith, whom everyone else called Grandpop, was charming, slightly hard of hearing, and wore a well-tailored suit. If Winnie had told either her grandfather or brother, he'd slept with her, they didn't seem to hold it against him. Victor Wolfe, in his mid-sixties, was urbane and charming, clapping Lorenzo on the back and asking him to pick out the wine. "Make it top-drawer," he said. "Even if it's wasted on some of these infants." Lorenzo did enjoy that part—like himself, Victor believed alcohol should be excellent and consumed responsibly. The somme-lier loved their party for that, and also loved the man-chil-dren, who drank less responsibly and had no problem saying, "What do you think, Vic? Another bottle?" to which Victor would respond, "Your livers won't thank you, but go ahead, boys."

Lorenzo indulged in one glass of Tenuta Casanova di Neri Cerretalto 2016 (blackberry and plum, dried cherry, tobacco, limestone, graphite and soil). He ordered chicken Milanese, since he'd already had red meat that month, and listened to Grandpop debate whether or not he should pop the question to his own significant other.

"While she is quite lovely, I don't fancy changing domiciles," he told Lorenzo. "Why, I might get lost in a new place! Or wander into someone else's yard. I can do that in Wellfleet. They all know me. The other day, in fact, I wandered over to the school during recess! My great-granddaughter was there, and believe it or not, the child didn't know how to double Dutch. Happily, I still do! Granted, my knee gave out, and I collapsed in a heap, but the little children were very kind, and of course I knew the first responder, and we ended up going out for lunch rather than the hospital."

Lorenzo was grateful for the old man's meandering tales. All he had to do was nod and make humming noises. Across the table, he watched as Austin, the head man-child, put his arm around Winnie's shoulders and brayed with laughter. Winnie, he noted, smiled.

He should not have found that irritating.

When they were done, Lorenzo was instructed to get back into the rented van, the garish, embarrassing kind with neon lights and loud, awful music. Worse, everyone was singing about bringing sexy back. Even Grandpop. Lorenzo felt hives forming on his neck. Would it be too rude to put his hands over his ears? Or to feign illness?

They were dropped off at a mini-golf course, broke into smaller groups and hit the balls through giant rabbit legs and under a windmill. It was fine. Lorenzo employed a little calculus and won within his group (the one that didn't have

Winnie in it). Then it was into the arcade, the likes of which Lorenzo hadn't been in since he was roughly ten years old. More whooping and loud music and celebrating that Ms. Pac-Man had defeated her foes.

"Last stop is the best stop!" Austin bellowed as they once again got into the party van. "Glitter Grotto, here we come!" Many cheers ensued.

Oh, God. Not a craft place. He'd heard about those wine-and-paint places. Glitter? He'd have to strip down in the garage to ensure none got back into the house.

"Don't even think about abandoning me, brother," Dante said. "I need you to fight off the women for me." Yes. He imagined the Glitter Grotto attracted more women than men. His sisters would probably like a craft night. Maybe he'd get them a gift card.

Unfortunately, the Glitter Grotto was not a craft shop. It was a strip club, he learned as they pulled into the parking lot. A neon sign showed a woman wrapped around a pole.

Lorenzo lurched to a stop. "I'll call an Uber," he said to no one in particular, and turned to go.

"You are not leaving me alone with a bunch of nearly naked women," Dante said with a grin. "You know they'll come for me."

"Who could blame them?" said Winnie, looping her arm through Dante's.

"That's why you're my favorite sister-in-law," Dante said. "Don't tell the others."

"Are you kidding?" she said. "I'm texting them right now. Come on, Lorenzo, you can't bail now. If I can take it, so can you."

With a sigh, he followed. He could be home, working on the proposal for a self-sealing suture that would protect against leaks or micro-perforations in vascular repair. Instead, he was here, where watered-down cocktails, loud music, and soft pornography abounded.

Lorenzo obviously loved the female form; he was straight, he was a physician, he appreciated the aesthetic beauty of women. He just didn't want to see them sliding around on a pole of dubious cleanliness, or popping their asses in his face, or doing slow, painful-looking splits in their eight-inch heels.

If he wanted to think about naked women, he'd rather just picture Winnie in that big bed in San Francisco.

But ten minutes later, he was sitting at a bar he'd just swabbed down with an alcohol wipe (he always had two or three in his wallet), nursing a bottle of Sierra Nevada Pale Ale (twist-off cap, so the bartender hadn't touched it).

"*She's* very graceful," said Grandpop, who was sitting to Lorenzo's left. "I wonder if she studied ballet. Young lady, are you perhaps a ballerina for your day job?"

"Ahn't you a dahlin'," said the woman in a thick Worcester accent. "Nope! I'm just naturally limbah."

"Well, here is twenty dollars for you, my dear. Congratulations on your many gifts!"

She bent down to kiss him on the cheek, and Lorenzo leaned as far away as humanly possible to avoid contact with her shoulder (or any other part). "Robert, I think I'll, um, check on Robbie," Lorenzo said.

"You do that," Grandpop said. "I'm rather enchanted by this lovely wood nymph here. What's your name, my dear?"

"Sapphyah."

"Sapphire? How unusual! And how creative your parents were to name you after a jewel."

"Welp, my real name's Mahtha. I just use Sapphyah on the stage."

"Very smart," Grandpop commended. "Martha is also beautiful name, but I see your point about anonymity. You know, if I were fifty years younger, I'd just ask for your phone number, Sapphire. You're a very hard worker!"

Lorenzo wove his way through the cheering bro-storm and finally spied Winnie, Robbie, Grady and Dante sitting at a table in the corner.

"Enough glitter for you, Lorenzo?" Robbie asked, grinning.

"More than enough. Your grandfather is having a wonderful time, however."

Winnie glanced over. "He's probably about to adopt her."

"Or marry her," Robbie said. "Winster, we wouldn't mind a step-grandmother younger than we are, would we?"

"Whatever makes Grandpop happy," Winnie said, clinking her bottle against his.

"Lorenzo, do you practice mostly at Mass General?" Grady asked, and Lorenzo was so, so grateful to talk about something normal. Grady had also gone to Harvard, he learned, though their paths hadn't crossed.

"Dr. Santini? Is that you? Oh, my God, wicked!"

Lorenzo turned and found himself eye-to-nipple with someone. Rather, eye to a nipple covered by a black leather studded thing five centimeters in diameter. In order to avoid being blinded (and sued), he jerked back, nearly toppling his chair. Robbie leaned forward and righted him, laughing.

"How do you know Dr. Santini?" Winnie asked, and her eyes were dancing with glee.

"I'm an intern at Cape Cod Hospital! This is amazing! Dr. Santini, listen. I hope I'm not being too forward—"

"You are," Lorenzo said, tilting his head to be as far away from her left breast as possible.

"I get it. You're celebrating something?" she asked.

"It's my bachelor party," Robbie said. "I take it you work here?"

"That's right. The tips are a lot better than at the ice cream stand, you know what I'm saying? My name's Greer Henderson, stage name Luscious. Nice to meet you and congratulations!" She leaned across the table to shake Robbie's hand, and this time Lorenzo had to slide out of his seat to avoid being hit in the face by her punk-rock pasties. In addition to the, ah, coverings, she wore a leather thong and ridiculously high heels. Her feet would be deformed before she was forty.

"Dr. Santini, I would kill to get into grand rounds with you," Greer said, looking up at him. Her eyelids were encrusted with glitter, and he could see a blob of glue on her false eyelashes. Glue, near the human eye. Ridiculous. "I'm just an intern, but I feel strongly that I'm heading for surgery. Do you have any advice?"

He glanced at his companions. "Yes. My advice would be not to approach me in public."

"That's cold, Lorenzo," Dante chided. "She's seizing an opportunity to pick your mighty brain. Now's as good a time as any, right?"

Later, he would kill his brother and apologize to Lark.

"Greer, sit down," Robbie said, and she did without apparent concern about the cleanliness of the chair.

"Lorenzo is an incredible mentor," Winnie said. "You were just talking about that in San Francisco, weren't you? Mentoring young medical students?"

He took a slow breath, turned to this Greer person and, looking only at her hairline, said, "Here's my advice, Dr. Henderson. Learn anatomy in theory and in practice. Think in three dimensions. Spend twenty minutes a day practicing suturing and knots, beginning now. Stop wearing those ridiculous shoes or you won't be able to stand for twelve hours in an OR. Listen to the nurses. They will know more than you for the next decade. Don't be defensive when criticized. Learn the instruments. Start training yourself to function on four hours or less of sleep. Show up early. Don't ask questions before trying to answer them yourself. Keep a journal of lessons learned from your mistakes and don't make them again. Best of luck."

Winnie, Robbie, Dante and Grady burst into applause. Greer said, "Thank you so much, Dr. Santini! I'm so glad I ran into you! Everyone's gonna be so jealous I got a one-on-one with Dr. Satan! Can I give you a hug?"

"No," he said. "Winnie, help me."

Winnie was laughing so hard tears sparkled in her eyes, and for a second, Lorenzo felt like smiling. She stood up, put herself between Greer and himself, and said, "Greer, if you really want to make a good impression on Dr. Santini, maybe don't mention we dragged him to a strip club for my brother's bachelor party, okay? He's here under duress, and only because he's a good guy."

"Oh, yeah, sure! I get it, a hundred percent." She looked at Lorenzo, and he quickly averted his eyes. "But can I sit in for grand rounds next time you're in Hyannis?"

The woman knew when to press an advantage, he'd give her credit for that. "Done."

"Heck yeah! Well, I've taken enough of your time," she said to the rest of the group. "Happy wedding! I'm sure she's a lucky woman, or he's a lucky man, or whatever. Mazel tov!"

"Robbie," Winnie said, "Lorenzo and I are leaving, okay? Enjoy the rest of the night, and keep in mind that it's already 1:30, so you should be heading home. Grady, don't let Grandpop spend our inheritance on tipping the ladies. Dante, you're perfect. Give Lark a kiss from me."

Then she took Lorenzo's hand and towed him through the bro-crowd and other patrons into the blissfully cold night air. The quiet was deafening in comparison.

"Want a raise?" he asked, but she just grinned, let go of his hand, which then felt strangely useless, and called them an Uber.

SEVENTEEN

WINNIE

Lorenzo had gone to give a speech in Houston, then stayed a few extra days to work with a colleague down there. He was due back tomorrow, and Winnie had spent the previous day in his Boston apartment, making sure the place was sparkling, refrigerator filled, laundry freshly done. She went to another condo association meeting for him, left him notes on the new pet policy (now allowed) and the increase in HOA fees. She made two arrangements of purple calla lilies and dark red roses with trailing eucalyptus leaves. Maybe she'd become a florist, she mused. Lorenzo had approved flowers as part of the budget, so even he liked them.

She'd also spent an afternoon with Joyce from 3B to see what her goals were. The gorgeous apartment was cluttered with forty years' worth of stuff, from years of old magazines to faded, poorly framed photos, dusty knick-knacks and dozens of plastic bins containing "things I think my kids might want." Winnie had made the usual list—keep, donate, toss—and reassured Joyce that her place would be much more welcoming and enjoyable without the clutter. She'd sent a text to Joyce's three kids, asking for a day when they could all come and claim any mementos before she got to work purging.

Now, she was in Wellfleet, in her own little house, which felt as warm and safe as a hug from Dad. Small, of course, and decidedly unglamorous. But she'd missed it just the same. Since she'd started working for Lorenzo, she'd only spent a couple of nights a week here. It terms of gossip, people had more or less moved on, and she barely needed to stare anyone down.

Now, she tugged on her running clothes—her body hated running, but her mind appreciated the blankness it offered. Besides, it was the quickest and most efficient way to stay fit. She started toward town, planning on making her usual loop of about three miles. The wind was cold off the water, and she was happy to make the turn onto Commercial Street, past the little shops and her mom's gallery, then onto Main Street, past the Marketplace and Preservation Hall. At Open Book, she stopped and went inside to visit Harlow. Their cousin, who was also Winnie's landlord, worked part time at the store, as well as Destiny, a full-timer who was standing on a ladder, cleaning the shelves.

"Hi, Winnie," she said.

"How's it going, Destiny?"

"Great, sweetie. How are you?"

"Fine. Killer dress, by the way," Winnie said. The outfits Lorenzo had bought for her had sparked an appreciation of quality clothing. "Cashmere?"

"It sure is. Twenty-two dollars on eBay."

"Sweet!" She paused. She'd never been into clothes a heck of a lot until she worked for Lorenzo. "Do you think we could sit down for half an hour sometime and you can give me some tips? I'm trying to up my wardrobe game.

Professional stuff, but also just looking better on the weekends and nights out."

"Sure," Destiny said. "I'd love to. And not to brag, but you're not the first person who asked me. Cynthia and I are going shopping next week. All the shops have marked down their stuff for the end of the season. You can tag along."

"Thanks! Maybe we can grab a drink afterward." Lorenzo wasn't the only one who could work on having more friends.

"I'd love that," Destiny said warmly.

"Is my sister around?"

"In the office doing the accounting."

"You mean, balancing the books?" Winnie said, raising her eyebrows.

"Very clever." Destiny smiled down at her, then resumed dusting. Winnie went through the warren of rooms and cozy spots. Grandpop was napping on the old leather couch, cuddled up with Ollie, Harlow's dog. Winnie stopped, covered them both with the knit throw, and went into the tiny office in the back.

"Hi, Harlow."

"Hey!" Harlow said, getting up and giving her a hug.

"I'm sweaty," Winnie said.

"As if I care. How are things? Heard Robbie's bachelor party was very robust."

"It was fun. Dinner was fantastic. I won at mini-golf, and Grandpop's new best friend is an exotic dancer named Sapphire. Thank God Grady and Dante were there as my fellow adults."

"And Lorenzo," Harlow added.

"Yep. Him, too."

Harlow waited. Winnie said nothing. Harlow waited

some more. She did this with all of her siblings, Winnie thought. Jedi mind tricks. That kind, lovely face, her gentle brown eyes.

"So you like him," Harlow said.

"Sure. He's easy to work for."

"Really? That's not his reputation."

"I'm not a doctor or a nurse. He's nicer to me." She felt her cheeks flush and figured she could blame it on the running.

"That's good to hear." Harlow smiled and gestured for Winnie to sit in the other chair.

"We slept together. One time." Damn those Jedi mind tricks.

"And?"

"Just...I don't know. It was surprising."

"In a good way?"

"In a very good way. But it was a mistake. I mean, he's my boss. We have nothing in common."

"Really? You sure?"

Winnie sighed. "I don't know. I..." She looked around and closed the office door with one foot. "I've been thinking about it a lot."

Harlow smiled. "Sure. You take that kind of thing very seriously."

"Yeah. I mean, we agreed it was a horrible idea. But in the moment, it was kind of...you know."

"Amazing?"

"Yes. Shit, Harlow. You should work as an interrogator for the FBI." Her sister laughed. "Anyway...never mind. It's a cut-and-dried case. Don't sleep with the boss. Sorry. I'm wasting your time."

"No, you're not! You're my baby sister. My favorite.

Don't tell the twins." She settled into her chair. "Listen, honey. That chef hurt you. You believed him, and he was a great liar. My guess is that he's very practiced in that area. It doesn't mean every relationship is going to break your heart."

"My heart is not in play," Winnie said.

"Mm-hm. Well, if it does come into play, keep that in mind. Sometimes relationships do work out. Sometimes they're pretty fantastic."

"Like you and Grady."

"Yep. And Lark and Dante. Mom and Dad. Destiny and Kate. Robbie and Rosie. Cynthia and Bertie."

"Now you're just depressing me." She took a deep breath, then exhaled. "It's not awful to stay single, is it?"

"Not if that's what you want."

"I've always been kind of a solo act."

"As much as someone with four siblings can be, sure. Doesn't mean that's carved in granite, though."

There had been a minute that night in San Francisco, somewhere in the wee hours after round two, where her head lay on Lorenzo's chest, and his hand had trailed through her hair. It had felt so...perfect. No real thoughts, just the sensation of *this feels right*.

But she'd had that sensation before. And both she and Lorenzo had almost immediately cut things off. Even if she had agreed, he thought it was a mistake. Best to kill any nascent thoughts of what-if.

"Yeah, I guess," she said. "Not carved in granite. But probably carved in something else very hard."

"Marble? Soapstone? Alabaster?"

"This is why you're the queen of trivia," Winnie said.

Harlow smiled, then reached out and touched Winnie's nose with her index finger. "Boop," she said.

Winnie smiled. Her oldest sister was magical as far as she was concerned. "Okay. Thanks for the talk. Love you."

"Love you too, honey."

With that, Winnie left the store, calling goodbye to Destiny. She texted Lark and Addison—

> Harlow said I'm her favorite sister, so suck on that, losers

then resumed her run in the chilly air. Tonight was the Santos anniversary party—the surprise sixty-fifth sweet Mr. Santos was throwing for his wife—and she had to get ready.

The event was at Preservation Hall, the lovely converted church that hosted events, weddings, and classes throughout the year. The guest list was relatively small—the Santos children, grandchildren and great-grandchildren, nieces and nephews, and a few longtime friends and neighbors. About thirty people. Mr. Santos had been the only person who hadn't canceled after she was declared the Outer Cape's scarlet woman. The only one. And since she'd been making bank as Lorenzo's assistant, she'd upped the budget for this little party. Better wine, food and flowers, nicer glasses and plates. She'd made a gorgeous bouquet for Mr. Santos to give his bride.

She showered, changed and loaded up her car with the flower arrangements she'd made last night, tablecloths and candles, wine and beer. The caterer was dropping off the food, one of Robbie's friends would be shucking oysters pulled fresh from the Atlantic this very day.

She didn't mind working alone. She liked it, even. But she did have to figure out a career. Lorenzo didn't really need a full-time assistant now that she'd found a house-cleaning service, scheduled window cleaners, rug and furniture steamers, the landscaping service, and a handyman service. Driving into Boston or Chatham to stock his fridge once a week was a bit silly. She could find someone local to do that.

As far as his calendar and travel management and the professional things he covered, she could do that remotely, and it would take a few hours a week at most. She could come to a conference again if he wanted, but after San Francisco, she doubted he would. Not just the sex-with-the-boss stuff. The telling-off-the-other-doctor stuff. The making-a-scene stuff. The trying-to-get-him-to-lighten-up stuff. Had she mentioned the sex-with-the-boss stuff?

Going back to event planning was out, courtesy of her Ice House speech. Florist? She'd have to take some serious classes for that. Maybe down the road, but it wasn't something she could just waltz into, and it would be very seasonal, as the bulk of Cape Cod weddings happened in the late spring and summer.

She *liked* being Lorenzo's PA. Liked his rigorous standards and love of detail. She liked trying to bring a little unexpected warmth into his magazine-worthy home. Seeing his surprise and pleasure at, say, that bottle of Icelandic liquor or the arrangement of gourds had made her heart feel very squishy.

She liked *him*. Of course she did. He was emotionally unavailable, decidedly single, married to his work, and uncomfortable with people on a personal level. What better choice? At least she'd stopped any fledgling flutterings in their itty bitty tracks. She was too sensible to fall in love with Dr. Satan, even if he was interested. And he had made it clear he was not.

TWO HOURS LATER, Mrs. Santos was crying happy tears as she danced with her creaky little husband, who stared at her as if it were their wedding day, dazed by his luck. Their kids were taking pictures, grandkids were smiling, the little great-grands dancing, too, yipping like happy puppies.

This would never be her, Winnie thought as she stood in the doorway. She was on track to have many nieces and nephews. She'd never longed to be a mother like Lark and Addie. She'd be the auntie, the childless one, available for babysitting and two desserts. Hopefully, Cynthia would let her rent the house forever, or maybe even leave it to her in her will (dubious, but one could hope). And somehow, she'd find a career that she loved. Maybe she'd move off Cape and wander through the country a bit, hitting all the cities she'd never seen, feeling that thrilling sense of potential.

Except she loved it here. If the current Baby Boomers were any example, her parents would live to be a hundred, and she could picture herself living with them, fixing their soup and taking them to various doctor appointments until she herself was an old woman, at which point her nieces and nephews would have to step up and at least visit her and arrange for her chin to be plucked. She'd have a series of increasingly smelly dogs. It didn't sound awful.

Speaking of dogs, poor Fluffina had appeared on the beach in Chatham the other day, her soft white fur dull and full of tiny burrs. Without a person to call, Winnie decided to take her into Lorenzo's house (what he didn't know wouldn't kill him). She washed and brushed the dog, blew her dry then spent another hour cleaning the bathroom (how much fur could a dog have? Good lord!). She called the town and left a message with Animal Control, asking if they might know who the owner was. Finally, she let Fluf-fina out, followed her down the beach until the dog had dashed off to her home. Winnie just wished they didn't leave her alone outside for so long.

"Winnie? What are *you* doing here?"

The voice startled her out of her grim reverie. It was Blakelee Johnson, dressed to kill in a velvet, tightfitting dress, a single and very chunky diamond pendant hitting the space between her collarbones. Was Mitchell-Tanner here? If Winnie saw him, would she be able to stop herself from punching him in the face? Dubious.

"I'm here with the kids," Blakelee said, correctly inter-preting Winnie's face. "Why are you here?"

"I'm the party planner," Winnie said.

"I'm surprised they hired you."

"Well, they hired me before you—before Nycholiss's birthday." She eyed Blakelee warily. "I take it you're related to the Santoses?"

"The groom, so to speak, is my great-uncle," Blakelee said.

"A very sweet man."

"Yeah, whatever." Blakelee scowled. "Look, Winnie. Uncle Tomas told me you charged them a hundred bucks for this. Is that true?"

"That's right," she said.

"That can't cover your costs."

"It doesn't. I donated a lot."

Blakelee's face was still hard. "Well. That was very generous."

"It was my pleasure." The memory of seeing Mitchell-Tanner at Logan flashed through her head. Those unkind, harsh words. How easily he mocked her for believing his lies, buying his Mitchell Prescott persona.

The man was a shit. And Blakelee was still with him. Maybe they deserved each other, or maybe...maybe Blakelee didn't have a lot of options. She didn't work, Winnie recalled. Times were tough, and divorces cost money (though that diamond pendant had to be worth a few thousand).

"Blakelee," she said, "I'm truly sorry. I swear I didn't know about you or the kids. I can't imagine how awful it must've been, finding out about me."

Blakelee's eyes flickered away. "Yeah. I thought all that was behind us. Hopefully, you were the last one." She toyed with the diamond. "I believe you, by the way. Sorry I made that big scene."

"It's okay."

"Mommy?" asked a little voice. "Will you dance with me?" It was Blakelee's littlest child.

"I would love to, sweetie!" Blakelee said, dropping her hand on her daughter's head. "Just give me another minute to finish talking to this nice lady, okay?"

"Okay," the little girl said. "Bye!" She skipped away, and Winnie could see the love on Blakelee's face shining.

It must be exhausting, being married to a guy like Tanner.

"Did you ever think about divorce?" Winnie blurted. Not that it was her business, but...

"Of course. You're his last chance. If he cheats again, he's out."

Winnie tried very hard not to move her face. That woman at the airport was not proof, after all. But Blakelee must've seen something, because her expression softened into sadness. A long moment passed. "Should I call my lawyer?" she asked quietly.

"I...I mean, it couldn't hurt," Winnie said. "Just so you know your options."

"Are you two back together?" Blakelee asked, her eyes suddenly shiny.

"No. Absolutely not."

Blakelee sighed. "I guess it's just a matter of time, to be honest. Want to know the irony? I'm his second wife. *I* was the other woman once upon a time. I thought things would be different with *me* because I was the love of his life. Stupid, right?"

"Everybody can be stupid. I think it's part of being alive."

Blakelee shrugged. "I guess. Again, sorry I ruined your business."

Winnie almost laughed at her blithe tone. "Yeah, no worries. I guess my heart wasn't really in it, anyway." Otherwise, she wouldn't have delivered that soliloquy at the Ice House.

"Well, you did a great job tonight," Blakelee said, waving her hand at the party. "Thanks for being so nice to Uncle Tomas and Aunt Grace." She paused. "If you need help covering the cost, we'd all pitch in."

"That's okay. It really was an honor." She looked at the woman in front of her, the tired eyes, the downturned mouth. "Take care, Blakelee. Good luck."

"Thanks." Blakelee walked away. Her little girl came up and tugged her onto the dance floor, and Blakelee scooped her up into her arms and onto the dance floor, smiling. She was a good mom.

When everyone had left, Winnie cleaned up, clearing off tables, scraping plates, and folding tablecloths. She was glad to see there was one flower arrangement left...she could give it to her mom. She was just about to start breaking down the tables when the door opened, and in came her brother. "Hey, Window. Figured you could use some help. Maybe we can grab some food afterward."

Maybe she would never find a partner. Good thing she had the family she did.

EIGHTEEN

LORENZO

He'd asked Winnie to come to Boston to arrange a party for the surgical residents and other staff he worked with. He was chief of special surgeries, after all, and other department heads did this kind of thing around the holidays. Why, he wasn't sure. The staff would all surely rather have a raise, or extra time off, than dinner with their work colleagues. He'd requested pay increases in the budget, but those things were decided later. Verline, the best charge nurse on Surgical, had strongly suggested the party, so a party would be thrown. And who better to arrange it than Winnie?

Also, it was a good excuse to see her. He hadn't been down to the Cape since her brother's bachelor party, and he'd been jammed with surgeries. This party gave him a great reason to get her here.

She emailed a list of questions—how many people would be invited, what kind of venue he wanted, what kind of food, all that—and he told her to make it nice enough so people would be glad they came. Honestly, he had no idea what would constitute a good party, but Winnie would.

> I have surgery until about four. Let's meet
> at the apartment after that.

> Sounds good.

Maybe they could get dinner together. Maybe it would be dark and late enough that she'd want to spend the night in Boston. Not in his bed, but just...well, in his bed would've been fine, if the situation had been different. But it wasn't, and he should get over it. Sex was one thing. A relationship was another. He didn't know how to do relationships. He'd tried twice, and both times the women had broken up with him in under a month. He hadn't felt it was worth pursuing, because each woman, while intelligent and attractive, hadn't affected him enough to think more on it.

But the thought of a night talking to Winnie was different. Calming. Relaxing. Energizing, too. Her smile. Her sass. Her complete lack of fawning. Her ability to take him at his word, not try to read into things or dissect his thoughts. The way she seemed to like him just as he was. Her fascinating eye color. The slight dimple that occasionally appeared when she smiled.

On the appointed day, he texted her when he left the hospital ninety-seven minutes later than he'd hoped.

> Meet me at the Hatch. Dropping you a
> pin now.

He left the hospital, pulling his wool coat over his scrubs. Usually, he showered and dressed in his street clothes, not wanting to be one of the masses who wore scrubs outside the hospital, but the surgery had run long, and he didn't want to waste time. It was already growing dark as he headed to the iconic shell, home of the Boston Pops July 4th concert, among others.

There she was, dressed in a parka and winter hat. She waved, and he felt his whole being lighten.

"Hi," he said.

"Hi, Satan," she said. "How was your day?"

Was it weird that he really liked her calling him Satan? "Good. How was yours?"

"Excellent. Let's walk and talk, since it's so nice out."

It was cold and getting darker, but he wasn't about to argue.

"So there's good news and bad news," she said. "Since you've left this to the very last minute, we're kind of limited in venues. Most places are booked, so next year we should start planning this in about August."

It was nice to think they'd be doing something together next year.

"But for this year, we can either do something at your place—"

"No," he said.

"—but I figured you'd hate that, so I looked into Sunday brunch—"

"Who would want to take time out of their weekend for a work event, even one with food?"

"—but I assumed no one would want to take time out of their weekend for a work event, and please stop interrupting, Lorenzo."

"Sorry." He almost smiled, though he wasn't sure why.

She narrowed her eyes at him, though she didn't seem irritated. "Which left me with the idea of a dinner cruise on the Charles." She headed into Fiedler Field, veering past the playground toward the dock.

"A dinner cruise sounds a little...cheesy."

"It does," she said. "But I'm about to blow your mind, so be patient." She went out on the dock. "For one, a dinner cruise has a two-hour time limit on it. Everyone has to disembark at the end, so there would be no lingering."

"I like that aspect," he said. The wind gusted off the river. "Won't it be too cold, though?"

"For two, it'll probably be wicked cold, which will keep people inside the boat. Huge windows, nice and toasty, and no one gets drunk and falls overboard."

"Another plus," he said.

"For three, look at that skyline. I mean, it's not Manhattan, but it's not ugly, either." She indicated Boston, and he had to agree. It was no Manhattan. "The food on the ship is supposedly five-star, and there's a really nice bar area. It won't be horrible."

"No," he said, looking down at her. "I'm sure it won't. Book it."

"I already did." She smiled at him, and he was fairly sure he was about to smile back. And maybe kiss her. Or fire her and then kiss her. Or give her a raise and then kiss her.

Thoughts of kissing were abruptly aborted, however.

"Mommy! Mommy, *Mommy!*"

Children. Maybe Winnie was right, and they did terrify him. This one's screams certainly did.

"Elliott!" came a woman's cry. "Oh, my God, Elliott, what are you *doing?* Sit down! How did you get—sit down, I said!"

"Well, shit," Lorenzo said. Because his surgeon's brain had already computed what was happening, and what would happen next, and it involved him and hypothermia, and even as he was shrugging out of his coat, he knew what had happened.

The child had been at the playground, no doubt, and had

wandered out onto the wide Fiedler dock. Some idiot had left a kayak tied there. The child, approximate four years old based on size and pitch of voice, had climbed in, and either the rope was insufficiently knotted, or the child had untied it, but that didn't really matter, because the kayak was now about ten yards off the dock, and Lorenzo was already running so that when he dove in the river, he'd be as close to the boat as possible. "Call 911," he ordered, and he imagined Winnie was already doing just that. There was the end of the dock, and then he was in the air, and then the achingly cold water swallowed him.

He heard the rush of water, surfaced, his head already in a vice of cold. He checked his distance to the child, heard the screams of the mother, and, though it might have been wishful thinking, caught the sound of Windsor Smith's calm, authoritative voice.

He swam—memories of him and Obasi laughing and clinging to the edge of their two-person scull, a mandatory drill for Harvard's rowing team. Then again, that had been in September, not late November. He was losing feeling in his legs.

His hand gripped the edge of the kayak. Elliott saw him and screamed. "Mommy! Help!"

"I'm helping," Lorenzo said, even as his teeth started chattering. "Sit down, please. I don't want you to fall in."

But the kid looked terrified and leaned further away, causing the kayak to tip.

"Grab on to the nice man!" his mother screamed from the dock. "He's a nice, nice man! He's not a stranger-danger man, Elliott! Hold on to him, honey. I know you're scared and your emotions are valid, but Mommy will be so proud if you hold on to him! You can have extra dessert if you sit down and hold on to the nice man!"

Parents today. So ineffective. Lorenzo heard a siren in the distance and idly wondered if his brother might be working today, or if Boston Fire did water rescues, or if that would be the Coast Guard.

Hypothermia tended to slow brain function.

"Sit down, Elliott," he said. But Elliott did not, just leaned out further, defying physics. Lorenzo pulled down on his side of the kayak to counterbalance it. He tried to boost himself in, but the angle and the cold prevented that. If the kid went into the river, Lorenzo was not sure he could save him. So he lunged up as best he could, grabbed the kid's ankle and held fast.

"He's getting me!" Elliott screamed. "Help me, Mommy!"

"I'm actually helping you right now," Lorenzo said. His whole body was shaking. The kid started kicking him. Really, the lack of gratitude. "Stop, Elliott," he said, but his voice was hard even for him to understand, given the chattering teeth.

"Elliott. Sit down," came a voice. A voice that took no shit. "Right *now*."

Elliott sat, whimpering

"Good boy," Lorenzo said. Otherwise, he had no plan. Freeze to death while waiting for help appeared to be the best he could do.

Something hit him on the head. "Sorry," said Winnie. Somehow, she also had a kayak, but cleverly was *in* hers, not clinging to it. "Can you hang onto the rope? I'll paddle us back to the dock." She indicated the line tied to the stern, which had just bumped into his head.

"I'm afraid to let go," he said. Elliot made another lunge, trying to get away from Lorenzo.

"Elliott, if you don't stay right there, Santa Claus will *not* come to your house this year. You understand me?"

"Yes," came the little voice. He settled back onto the seat.

Winnie maneuvered the kayak around Lorenzo, looped the rope under one of the bungee cords that crisscrossed the top, and tied it. Lorenzo saw flashing red lights—a fireboat approaching. His odds of not dying had just risen.

"Hey, there. How you doin'?" said a firefighter.

How were they *doing*? Not well.

"The kid is fine," Winnie called. "This guy probably has hypothermia. Probably faster if I just paddle them back to the dock."

"Sounds like a plan," said the firefighter. "Love me a logical woman."

Three minutes later, two of Boston's bravest were hauling Lorenzo onto the dock. An EMT wrapped him in a silver foil blanket, Elliott was sobbing in his sobbing mother's arms, and Winnie was being asked out for a beer. "You know what they say about firemen," the guy was saying. "We know how to use a hose."

"I know exactly what they say about firemen. You're either husbands or whores. I'm guessing you're the latter."

"It's like we met before," the guy said, his voice admiring.

"You wanna give a statement?" another firefighter asked, the one who was actually doing something helpful. "Actually, do I know you? You look familiar."

"We've never met," Lorenzo said. "And no. I live close by. I'd like to go home."

Winnie came over, helped him on with his coat, since he was shuddering too hard to do it alone. "My hero," she said.

"Actually, you're mine. Thank you for saving my life."

"Guys, I recorded the whole thing," said a kid about twenty. "Uploading it to TikTok right now!"

"You were recording?" Winnie asked, whipping around. "While he was freezing to death trying to save a *kid*? Did you think about helping, you little shit, or was going viral more important?" She grabbed his phone and threw it in the Charles. "Oops."

Well, if Lorenzo hadn't loved her already, he sure loved her now. He was too tired to argue with that fact.

A police officer, also on the scene, obligingly dropped them off at his apartment, and Lorenzo got in the shower, the hot water like needles at first. He stood there until feeling returned to his fingers and toes, then washed off whatever bacteria the Charles had gifted him. He pulled on a cashmere jogging set he'd bought in Italy the year before and walked down the hall.

Winnie was in the kitchen, cooking something that smelled fantastic. He looked at her for a long minute. Maybe he could claim the need for skin-to-skin warming.

Then his phone buzzed. A text from Verline.

> Dr. Santini, we have a mass casualty here, city bus vs. dump truck, rolled down an embankment. Cabrera, Hussein and Brooks are all here, but we need you, too.

No cozy night in, then.

> On my way.

"Looks like I have to go," he said. "Big accident."

"Seriously? You should let someone else handle it, Lorenzo. You must be exhausted."

"I'll be fine."

"You're not God, Satan. Sorry to tell you, you're a mere mortal."

He smiled. "God-like, anyway, at least in the OR. I'm not sure how long I'll be. I might sleep at the hospital."

She paused. "Okay. I get it. They'll be lucky to have you."

"See you in the morning?" he asked, pulling on his coat once more.

"It's my grandfather's birthday tomorrow," she said.

So no, in that case.

He went over to her, wrapped her in his arms, and kissed the top of her head. "Great work today. And I'm not talking about the dinner cruise."

She hugged him back. Hard. For a second, he just held onto her, wishing he could stay exactly where he was. Then, reluctantly, he pulled back and headed back out into the cold New England night.

NINETEEN

WINNIE

She had to do something about Lorenzo. Something *for* him, maybe.

He'd been running down the dock before she even saw the kid in the kayak. She had never seen anything so brave, but even more than that, he did it without a single thought about himself. Who dives into the Charles River in late November when it's twenty-eight degrees out?

No one else, that's who.

She knew she'd done all the right things, too—on with 911 before he reached the boat, giving the location, telling them to send a boat and an ambulance. But even with the excellent response rate of the Boston Fire Department, she hadn't been willing to wait. The kid was trying way too hard to get away from Lorenzo. What if he went overboard? There'd be a good chance he would drown, and Lorenzo might die trying to save him, and Winnie might also die trying to save him, and the mother would also probably try to save her son, and the Charles would be littered with bodies.

So she did what she was good at. Our most competent

child, her parents liked to say, and she knew she was mani-festing that a thousand percent at that moment. She spotted the other kayak, ran down to it and climbed in, grateful she'd spent all those times with Harlow paddling around the bay. Then she ordered Elliott to sit down *now* and got to Lorenzo as fast as she could. Regretted bumping his head, but at least she was there.

The whole thing had taken maybe eight minutes from Lorenzo running down the dock to being pulled out of the water. Her own legs were shaking by then, but out of fear. The sight of the little boy in his mother's arms...God.

Then there was the sight of Lorenzo, dripping, shaking, ice forming in his hair, his face pale. He looked up at her and smiled, and her heart just about threw itself out of her chest at him.

While he was thawing out in the shower, she started making a hearty chicken stew. She'd have him drink some whiskey with honey, too. She'd make sure he ate a hearty meal, then tuck him into bed...and crawl in with him, maybe. For comfort and warmth only, (cough). Unless he felt otherwise, at which point shagging the boss made a whole lot of sense.

She sure hadn't pictured him going to the hospital.

After he left, she finished making the stew, baked some cornbread with jalapenos, then baked a batch of cookies (with sugar she'd stashed in his pantry for the times she stayed over). She waited up as long as she could, hoping to hear him in the hallway. The events of the evening caught up with her, though...all that adrenaline and terror...so when her eyes burned and her lids grew heavy, she went down the hall to the guest room.

When she woke up around seven, he was still gone. She wished she could skip Grandpop's birthday. But what if it was Grandpop's last birthday? They'd all been thinking that for the past fifteen years, granted, but one of these years, it would be true. She started to send Lorenzo a text, but his notifications were silenced. Could be he was still in surgery, or maybe sleeping, so she wrote a note instead.

Dear Dr. Satan, Hero of the Charles—
I hope you'll get a lot of sleep today. I left chicken
stew in the fridge and made some cornbread and
cookies because people who save children get to have
carbs.
What you did yesterday was amazing. I'm so proud
of you.
~ Winnie

She thought about scrapping it because of that last sentence, but hell. The man deserved to be told. And maybe told more than just that she was proud of him.

But he was still her boss.

Then, regretfully, she gathered up her things and left.

TWENTY

LORENZO

Thankfully, the millennial at the dock was the only one who appeared to have been filming Elliott's rescue, because no one said anything to Lorenzo about his adventure in the river. He texted Dante to ask if he'd heard about a child rescue on the Charles, and Dante had said yes, a little kid had gone adrift, but a good Samaritan had saved him.

> Why?

his brother asked.

> Did you treat anyone at the hospital? I
> heard there were no injuries.

> One of my coworkers witnessed it.

> I was just curious.

Winnie had checked in after her grandfather's birthday party. Asked if he needed anything from her. Unfortu-nately, he couldn't think of anything, professionally speaking. Plus, his calendar was booked solid with surgeries and grand rounds.

What to do about Winnie. The thought was keeping him up at night, literally, and he hated that. If he wanted to date her, he should fire her, which didn't seem very fair. Then, if he did fire her, was it ethical of him to say, "By the way, any interest in dating me?" Probably not. And even if it was, what if she said, "Didn't we cover this already? That was a mistake, Lorenzo. Thanks, anyway." She may well have started dating someone on the Cape. So if he kept her as his assistant, he'd get to see her. At least there was that.

He finally found a gap in his schedule to go to Chatham for the weekend. Surely he could find a reason to get Winnie to come to his place, though she was far too efficient these days. Could he ask her to paint a few rooms? That would take some time, wouldn't it? Or would she just hire that out?

"You're coming down?" his mother exclaimed when he called her. "Wonderful. Come on Thursday. Family dinner here, Friday at six. Bring wine." Then she'd ended the call before he could object.

He loved his family. But God, he was tired. He texted to ask her to move it to Sunday so at least he could have a couple of days of down time...well, time to work on that suture he wanted to finish. But she ignored his messages, as did mothers everywhere when they didn't want their children to dodge their plans.

When he drove home on Thursday, it was a physical relief to walk into his house. He loved his Boston apartment, but this...this was home. Winnie had been there—the thermostats were set at the exact temperature he liked. A few vases of white roses and eucalyptus leaves cheered the place up. In the kitchen, on a cake platter covered by a glass dome, were a dozen chocolate chip cookies with a note: *Live a little, Satan.*

He was running out of things for Winnie to do. The dinner cruise was all set, and it seemed that people were looking forward to it. The holidays were around the corner —his least favorite time of year, with all the tacky décor in the hospital, the constant bleating of Christmas carols sung by pop stars of varying talent, the pressure to have fun and accept invitations. He could probably foist off some gift-buying and check-writing duties on her—he had to give gifts to his surgical team, the med/surg nurses, his family. Come January, though, he wondered if she'd want to move on. She was the type to want a purpose, a project.

But for now, she was still his personal assistant.

Hm. Maybe she could assist him tomorrow night at his family dinner. In a rare move, he called her number, rather than send a text.

"Hello?" she said.

"I need some help at an event tomorrow night. A dinner."

"Hello to you, too, and where is this dinner? Boston or Chatham?" she asked.

"Chatham. Can you be here by five?"

"I *can*, Dr. Santini, in that I have the ability to drive there by the appointed hour. Shall I make that commitment?"

He felt himself smile. "Are you making fun of my grammar?"

"I am."

He was a little surprised by the burst of warmth in his chest. "Yes, please make that commitment, Ms. Smith." He hesitated, not quite wanting to hang up. "The cookies were unnecessary. I'll probably throw them out."

"How dare you? Have you had one? To taste one is to know God."

"I'm an atheist." That warmth increased pleasantly.

"I don't believe that for one second. Is there a dress code for dinner?"

"Yes. Look nice."

"I always look nice. You, on the other hand, have resting bitch face. Have a great night." She ended the call.

Yes. He was definitely smiling. He looked at the cookies again. There was absolutely nothing that was good for a human in those ingredients. He took the lid off, picked one up and inhaled the scent of chocolate and butter and some kind of nut. Peanut butter, maybe? That would explain the lighter-colored chips.

One bite wouldn't kill him. He closed his eyes as the flavors flooded his mouth. Maybe he didn't know God, but *damn*. That was a good cookie. Gone before he knew it.

Another one wouldn't kill him.

THE NEXT EVENING, Winnie arrived at the requested time, an hour before his mother had ordered him to come. "Hi! How are you?" For a second, he thought they might hug. They'd saved a child's life together, after all. They'd hugged that night.

But the moment passed. Her hair was in its usual smooth ponytail, and for a second, he remembered how it had felt to tug her hair free and slide his hands through it. How it fell like water down her back, how it smelled like flowers and rosemary, how it had felt brushing against his face when she'd rolled on top of him—

"What?" he asked.

"How are you, Lorenzo?" she repeated patiently, tilting her head.

"Fine." She wore a sack-like brown knit dress with darker brown boots. A sloppily tangled necklace of pearls and gold strands looked like a child had made it. She wore pearl earrings and a gold ring on her index finger. When had she started dressing with such...flair? "You look..."

"Great?" she suggested. "Lovely? Warm?"

"I didn't buy that for you," he said.

"You want to hear something crazy? I owned clothes before I met you. I also shop for myself occasionally."

"I know that. Obviously. You just look...different." He should stop talking now.

"I look perfectly presentable. Even lovely." Her voice was a command. "Is this not appropriate for the dinner?"

"It's fine. I just assumed you'd wear one of the outfits I bought for you."

"If you want something to dress up, buy a Barbie doll."

"I just asked you to look nice." Super. That did not come out the way he intended.

"I *do* look nice, Lorenzo," she growled. "You have one second to switch your tone and drop the topic, or I'm going to leave, or kick you."

"You look nice," he said. "Don't go. Sorry."

"Apology accepted. What is this dinner, anyway?" she said, fishing her iPad from her bag. "Do you want me to take notes? I gather it's a doctor thing?"

"It's a family thing."

She looked up. "Oh."

Right behind her were four of the remaining cookies. He wished he'd thrown them out so she couldn't see he'd eaten eight.

"Um...why do you want me at a family dinner?" she asked.

"Because I hate them. Family dinners, not the humans involved."

"You don't hate family dinners."

"Actually, I do, Winnie, and who would know better? You or me?"

"I would," she said. "Lorenzo. I know you feel like you don't fit in. But you do. Or you could. You're a truly good person. You should tell them about rescuing that little boy."

"Absolutely not."

"Why? They deserve to know that version of you. You're the one uncomfortable with it. It's easier for you to be distant than to be...vulnerable."

He remembered when, two summers ago, he'd seen Dante's smashed-up truck during a pileup on Route 6, the panic that had shot through him at the thought of his little brother, hurt. His brother had been fine, but for those few seconds...

"I'm fairly sure I didn't hire you for a personality analysis," he said to cover the fact that she was absolutely right.

"Yet you get it for free. Maybe I should ask for a raise," she said, and there was a flash of her smile, that mysterious dimple.

He sighed. "You're not completely wrong. I do feel uncomfortable with them, and I wanted you to come tonight so you can be a buffer. You can talk to me so I don't have to engage."

"No, thank you."

"You work for me, Winnie."

"Yes, but I'm not a wind-up toy who does everything you command. This is your family. I'm your personal assistant, not your bodyguard. What's the worst that could happen? Your sisters will hug you? You might have to hold a baby?"

He rubbed his forehead. "I just..." He stopped because he didn't know how to explain. He hated that, not knowing.

"Just what, Lorenzo?" she asked, and her voice was a little gentler. She sat at the counter and gestured for him to do the same. He did.

"I...don't disagree with your assessment. I'm uncomfortable with them. I'm not—" he made air quotes— "one of them."

"Because you grew up with your grandmother, not them."

"Yes. And because I'm far more intelligent—"

"No, no. Shut that right down. You're not. You're just *differently* intelligent, okay? When we talk about emotional intelligence, you're a three, and they're all tens." She looked at him another long minute, and he shifted. "Why don't you tell them how you feel? At least get a little closure on that front."

"Closure is a myth," he said. After a beat, he added, "How would I do that?"

"Most of us use words, Satan. You could just say you wish you could be closer. That you don't know how to get past feeling like that lonely little boy who was sent off to school. You could tell them that you missed them. That you wished you had more chances to connect with them. That you've been overcompensating by throwing money around and staying one step removed because you're scared they'll—"

"Okay, that's enough. Forget I asked. Just...just come along. I'll tell them you were in town for business and I decided to bring you."

"I *am* in town for business. I'm on the clock and have been since I left my house."

He eyed the cookies, suddenly understanding the phrase *eating your feelings*. "Let's go, then. You're expensive."

"Worth every cent," she said, and he did not disagree.

———

AN HOUR LATER, they were all seated around the giant dining room table in his parents' house. Everyone had gone a little crazy when they saw her, practically trampling him to hug her. "I didn't know you were coming!" Lark said, wiping away tears of joy at seeing her sister, though surely, it had been a matter of days since they last got together.

"Oh, my God, I *love* your dress!" Sofia had exclaimed, prying them apart for her own hug. His parents greeted her warmly, and then, finally, his mother hugged him and patted his cheek, Dante had brought him a beer, which Lorenzo didn't want. He was already sweating.

"The great man deigns to visit," Izzy said, and Lorenzo ignored her, as he always did when he sensed he'd be the butt of a joke. Sofia came over, William on her hip. "Say hello to Uncle Lorenzo, honey," she said, prying the child's arms off her neck to pass him.

"Hello, William," Lorenzo said, taking the reluctant boy. William screamed, then pitched himself backward, writhing, until Lorenzo put him down. William ran to his father and clutched his legs, sobbing as if Lorenzo had just bitten the head off a kitten.

"I think he hates me," Lorenzo observed.

"He doesn't *hate* you," Sofia said.

"I hate Lowenzo," William sobbed. "Make him go."

Now the food was served, wine was flowing (water for him) and the noise was deafening. Winnie was not being at all useful, just eating and talking to his family and getting them all to like her more than they already did.

"Brother, what stick is up your ass today?" Dante asked, his tone pleasant. "You've barely said a word."

"Yeah, Lorenzo. Why so quiet?" Izzy asked.

"Oh. I..." He looked at Winnie, who gave a nearly imperceptible nod. "I'm just tired," he said. It was a cop-out, but the thought of talking about feelings made him feel a little ill.

"Poor Dr. Satan," Izzy said. "Work is hell, I gather? See what I did there? Satan? Hell?"

"Leave him alone," Mom said. "He works so hard."

"I also work hard, Ma," Izzy said. "Harder, because I'm a nurse."

"Excuse me, I'm a teacher," Sofia said. "I have twenty-nine children in my class this year, and they're all feral."

"Yet they worship you," said Henry. "Queen of the feral children."

"Sorry," Dante said. "My wife is an ER doctor, busy sewing severed limbs back onto people." That wasn't true, Lorenzo knew, because obviously an orthopedic surgeon would do that. "Meanwhile," his brother continued, "I run into burning buildings and rescue babies and puppies, so I think we can agree that I win."

"All you kids work hard," Dad said. "You get it from your mother, who spent all day in the kitchen making this for you."

"It's amazing, Ma," Dante said. "Thank you."

Talk turned to their mother's cooking and talent. Lorenzo looked pointedly at Winnie. *See?* he wanted to say. *I told you this wouldn't work.*

"Actually, Lorenzo, why don't you...tell them that... thing?" Winnie suggested.

"What *thing*?" he growled. In other words, *no*.

"Are you two getting married?" his mother gasped.

"We are not, Mrs. Santini, but thank you for the joy in your voice just then." Winnie took a bite of eggplant and widened her eyes at him.

"I would kill to have you as a daughter-in-law," Anita said. "Lark, imagine that! Your sister *and* your sister-in-law!"

"That would be very unique," Lark said. She turned her kind eyes to Lorenzo. "What did you want to talk about, Lorenzo?"

The table quieted, more or less. William looked at him and whimpered.

Winnie looked at him steadily. *Go ahead*, she mouthed.

Lorenzo put down his fork and inhaled. "Well. Yes. I...I suppose I did want to bring something up." Everyone was looking at him. Sweat trickled down his back. "I've always felt a little...separate from the rest of you. Being sent to St. George's—"

"Oh, please, not this again," said his father. "Lorenzo. That was a gift. A privilege. Do you know how much we spent on that school? You *loved* it there. It was where you belonged. You didn't even want to come home for the holidays!"

"You aways wanted to stay with Noni," Sofia said.

"He was welded to Noni," Izzy said. "He used to tell me straight out that he was her favorite. Which was true. I don't think she ever fully understood that I was also her grandchild."

"I was seven at the time, Dad," Lorenzo said. "And yes, it was a stellar school, but I've always felt...somewhat... isolated because of that. From the rest of you."

"You mean, you don't *want* to be superior to the rest of us?" Izzy asked. "Isn't that kind of your thing, though? Telling us how much smarter and better you are?"

His shirt was now stuck to his back. "No. It's not my thing."

"Well," Dante said. "It's *been* your thing, brother."

"I'm trying to say that...sometimes...I feel..." *Wistful. Lonely. Envious.*

"Bitter?" Izzy offered.

"Resentful," he snapped. "Because you're all this big happy pile of puppies, and I was sent away and became who I am and now just pay for college and weddings and houses and vacations, and no one here really even..." Shit. This was going horribly.

"Lorenzo, maybe you could be a tiny bit more diplomatic?" Sofia said. "Everything you just said, you gave to us without anyone asking. You offered. You're very generous, and we've all thanked you many times."

"Do you want us to put up a statue?" Izzy said. "Maybe carve your face into the side of Mom and Dad's house? Would that be good enough?"

"Harsh, Izzy," Dante said.

"Me? Are you kidding?"

The conversation was sinking faster than the *Titanic*. "No! I'm trying to say I...I just wish I hadn't been...sent away." For a second, it was like he was in the back of Noni's car, looking out the back window as his family grew smaller and smaller, Noni's stream of Italian meant to make him feel better and somehow making him feel worse.

His mother threw down her napkin. "Are you going to *criticize* us, Lorenzo? We did what we thought was best! We *sacrificed* for you! Do you think it was easy sending you off to that school? Do you think my heart wasn't broken every night when I saw your empty bed? You were too smart for a regular school, and when your grandmother told us about St. George's, it seemed like the best thing for you. And here you are, ridiculously successful, but now we were bad parents?" She burst into tears.

"I didn't say that," Lorenzo said, rubbing his forehead. Why had he listened to Winnie? Why?

"You made your mother cry," said his father. "Nice work. She worked all day on this meal, and God knows how long it's been since we all got together, and you're bringing this up, Lorenzo? You're forty-one years old. Get over it. Honey, please don't cry. Come here." His father wrapped an arm around his mother and glared at Lorenzo.

No one said a thing. William then joined his grandmother and started wailing. Lorenzo glanced at Winnie, who looked frozen, then down at his plate.

Dante cleared his throat and said, "Well, completely meaning to change the subject..." He took Lark's hand. "Mom, Dad, you're gonna have another grandchild."

There was a beat of silence, then the room exploded with shrieks and shouts and congratulations. For one second, Lark caught his eye and smiled, and Lorenzo gave her a nod. Happy news for sure, and not surprising. Winnie yelped with joy and hugged her sister, and Sofia was telling William he would be a big-boy cousin, and Izzy ran downstairs to the wine cellar that Lorenzo had stocked for his father for his sixty-fifth birthday and brought up champagne, and the rest of the night was all about baby names and breastfeeding and cervixes.

Lorenzo didn't have much to add other than congratulations. He hugged his brother, kissed Lark on the cheek, got his mother champagne and felt like a criminal.

An eternity later, Lorenzo and Winnie got in his car and headed for home.

"We're going to have a niece or nephew," she said happily. "Wow. I'm not a hundred percent surprised, but it's such great news. They're coming to Wellfleet tomorrow to tell my side of the family. They'll be the best parents."

"Yes."

She looked at him, then straight ahead. "Sorry your talk didn't go well."

"It did not go well. You are correct."

That was all the conversation they had for the next fifteen minutes. His jaw was locked with frustration. When they pulled into his driveway, he said, "You're welcome to spend the night." Then, because that sounded too suggestive, he added, "Downstairs, of course."

"Yeah, I knew that." She tilted her head to look at him. "What? You clearly want to tell me something."

"Your advice was *disastrous*," he said. "I wish I hadn't listened to you."

"It didn't land right, that's for sure. I'm sorry."

"It was *disastrous!*" he repeated. "No one wants to hear anything from me. It doesn't matter how I feel, because apparently, I'm not allowed to have feelings. I have a successful career, and I should never ask for anything, even if it's just to feel a little less like a stranger in my own family."

Her face softened, and she put a hand on his forearm. "Oh, Satan," she said. "I'm sorry."

"You should be! I don't know why I thought you would have something intelligent to offer."

"Wow. That's *really* rude."

"Well, Winnie, you don't know them, do you? You don't

know *us*. It's very clear no one in my family cares that there were aspects of my childhood that...left a mark."

"It's not that they don't care, I bet. Besides, it's important to say those things anyway, even if you don't get the response you want."

"Why?" he demanded. "So I could be insulted and dismissed?"

"Well, no. But I guess you have to accept what they can and can't give and let it go."

"Where was that advice before, Winnie? I thought I was supposed to pick my scabs and tell them how I felt. But now it's 'let it go'? Can you stick with just one pop psychology theory, please?"

She winced. "I'm sorry. I am, Lorenzo. I'm sorry you didn't get what you wanted."

"I *have* what I want! Look around, Winnie! I'm very successful! I have everything! Life has worked out extremely well for me, in case you didn't notice."

Was that pity on her face? Pity? "It's okay to want more, Lorenzo. To connect with people. To let them see more than one side of you. And you could, if you'd just get out of your own way."

The pressure in his head made it feel like his eye was about to pop out of the socket. "You know what?" he said, his voice flat. "You're fired."

She blinked but said nothing.

"You think I'm someone I'm not, and it's maddening," he went on. "What about your own life? You've spent years underachieving career-wise, you chose an idiot to fall in love with, and somehow you feel qualified to lecture me on how I'm doing. It's condescending and tone-deaf."

Her face turned stony. "*I'm* condescending and tone-deaf?"

"Thank you for your work. I'll pay you for the whole night, and you can stay here if you've had too much to drink—"

"I had a ginger ale and water."

"Good. Then you can drive home."

"Fine. I'll expect a glowing reference." She got out of the car, then bent down, her ponytail slipping over her collarbone. "And you're right about the idiot I chose to fall in love with." Then she slammed the door of the Lamborghini as hard as the car would allow.

TWENTY-ONE

WINNIE

He was the idiot she'd fallen in love with. The second one in a row. Her heart felt like a shriveled piece of seaweed.

Obviously, his talk with his family didn't go so well. But fired? Yes. Fired. Once again, she was unemployed. She drove very carefully to make up for the chaos in her head.

But it was okay. It was *fine*. Ir wasn't like the job had long-term prospects. The end had been coming no matter what. He had just made it...definitive. It was *fine*.

When she got home, there was a letter of recommendation in her inbox. For God's sake, he sure hadn't waited long to sever their last tie.

To Whom it May Concern:
Windsor Smith served as my personal assistant for
the past three months. As a surgeon with an
extremely demanding clinical, academic and admin-
istrative schedule, I relied heavily on her exceptional
organizational skills, judgment and intelligence, all
of which she consistently exhibited throughout her
employ. She handled complex scheduling, confiden-

tial medical and professional correspondence, travel logistics, as well as high-level coordination with hospitals, academic institutions, and professional organizations, always with efficiency and professionalism. I found her to be a person of deep integrity and a strong work ethic, and she has my unequivocal recommendation.

Sincerely,

Lorenzo Santini, M.D., Ph.D.

Chief of Special Surgeries at Mass General Brigham Hospital

Distinguished Professor at Harvard University Medical School

Fellow of the American College of Surgeons

She wondered if he'd asked ChatGPT to write it, since it was so impersonal. Then again, so was he.

Even as she had the thought, she felt a little ashamed. He was not impersonal. She knew that, maybe better than anyone. The image of him fresh from the Charles flashed like a razor. Was she crying? Shit. She was crying. She stomped around her tiny house for half an hour, opening and closing cupboards before finally going to bed with four *Dateline* podcast episodes in the queue to soothe her battered heart.

She felt calmer the next morning. The pragmatic child of Gerald and Ellie Smith had things to do. A résumé to polish. Rosie and Robbie's wedding in two weeks. Her house could use a good scouring. She had another session with Joyce, Lorenzo's disorganized neighbor, in Boston.

He'd been so angry. Hurt, really, but also so angry. Had she really been so wrong to urge him to talk to his family? Maybe he was right. She didn't know them.

She did, however, feel like she knew *him*. The man who had so capably looked after her when she'd run into Mitchell at Logan Airport. Who had kissed her in the elevator, who had jumped into a river to save a little boy and then gone back to the hospital and saved someone else's life. He was a man of few words, but God, the words he had said mattered so much. The soft ones *and* the hard ones.

Her heart ached. He was right. Her advice had not done anything but upset his parents and disappointed him. What did she know? She was the invisible one, after all. She'd never brought *that* up during a family dinner. Why had she thought Lorenzo should?

Maybe because it mattered to him so much, whereas she was pretty okay with her role.

And also...maybe she wasn't as invisible as she'd once thought. Quieter, maybe. Less of a drama queen than Addie and Robbie, less brilliant than Harlow and Lark, but she'd never felt unimportant. She knew she was loved.

Maybe Lorenzo didn't. Maybe that was the difference.

After the Smith family had done a similar joy-explosion at Lark and Dante's news, Winnie waited a few days, then drove down to meet Lark after her shift in the ER. They went to a little pub near Hyannis Hospital, one that offered half-pound cheeseburgers and fried pickles, a place Winnie was sure Lorenzo would never visit.

Her sister was waiting for her. They hugged, ordered their burgers, talked about how Lark was feeling, how they were both so excited to see their nephew at the wedding, and how long Grandpop's best man speech was.

And then, as they ate their delicious and unhealthy meals, Winnie got to it.

"Lorenzo fired me."

"Oh, no! I'm so sorry! He's not easy to work for, I'm sure."

"Actually, he was pretty great. I loved the job, and he was a very good boss."

Her sister took an enormous bite of her bacon and blue cheese burger. "So what went wrong, honey?" she asked thickly, cheeks bulging.

To her shock and horror, Winnie felt tears sting her eyes. "I, uh...I pushed him a little. To talk about his feelings and tell his family that he wished he felt closer to them. Because he's a little stunted, as you know, but underneath, he's...more."

"I always thought so, too," Lark said with a kind smile, then eyed the uneaten half of Winnie's burger. "Are you going to finish that?"

"No, no, go ahead."

Lark lunged. "Sorry, I'm starving. I swear, I eat seventeen times a day." When Winnie didn't respond, Lark said, "So why did he fire you?"

Winnie looked at her plate. "I told him he should get out of his own way, in a nutshell. That he could do better with people if he wasn't so afraid of rejection." Like it had been any of her business. "And he didn't like that assessment. I should've stayed in my lane. I don't blame him."

Lark finished the last bite of the burger. "Well, you weren't wrong," she said, swallowing. "Do you miss him?"

Winnie cut her a filthy look.

"Kind of fell for him, didn't you?"

"No!" She paused. "Maybe. Yes. Here, eat my fries, you poor starving thing."

Lark accepted. "So what now?"

"Now? Nothing. I'll see him at your baby's christening and once or twice a year after that."

"Mm." Lark said nothing else, using a few of Harlow's Jedi mind tricks. Robbie would've stolen her phone and texted Lorenzo pretending to be her. Addie would've given an hour-long lecture on how to be more like her and Nicole.

"So you're feeling pretty good?" Winnie asked, eager to change the subject. "I mean, Lark, there's a human growing inside you!"

"I know! I feel great. Just hungry all the time. Hey, speaking of christenings..." She paused and ate another fry, then smiled at Winnie. "Will you be our baby's godmother?"

Winnie choked. "Seriously? Addie will shiv me! But yes! Oh, my God, are you sure, Lark? What about Dante's sisters, though?"

"We both want you," Lark said.

A different kind of tears filled Winnie's eyes. "Yes. Of course. Thank you, Lark. But seriously, Addie's going to murder me in my sleep once she finds out. Pretty sure she thought her twinship would land her godmother."

Lark leaned across the table and kissed Winnie's cheek. "Believe it or not, she already knows."

"Should I check my brake lines?"

"Nope. She said it was a great idea."

"Once she stopped hissing and biting you, you mean?"

Lark laughed. "Yes. She's about to send you ten thousand suggestions of what the baby will need. Ignore them all."

"She can still buy you all the stuff. I mean, she is the queen of consumers."

"She is. Dante and I are happy with hand-me-downs, though. Maybe your job can be returning presents we don't want."

"Ah ha. It's all making sense now, this godmother

honor." But she smiled at her sister, touched beyond words. "Your baby will be the luckiest baby in the world because you're its mother, Lark," she said, and she meant it.

SHE HAD LEFT her favorite pair of pajamas at Lorenzo's Chatham house. She checked her phone to see where he was—he had yet to turn off location sharing. He was at Mass General, of course. She felt a pang at the image of him standing over a patient in the OR, solemn and focused and brilliant (and tired, misunderstood and lonely; knock it off Winnie, he's fine). At any rate, he was two hours away, and she could go to the house, get her jammies, take a final look at the house she'd come to love and say goodbye.

The place was chilly, though a few lights were on, since she'd set up daylight sensors so the place wouldn't look abandoned after dark. She went inside, down the stairs and past the wine-red couch, which she patted in farewell. Got her pajamas, checked to see if there was anything else of hers, ordered herself not to be sentimental, because her throat was tightening. This place had been a shelter for her, a place to be useful and heal. The sheets on her bed were already clean, all the towels fresh, so she had no excuse to stay longer. Back upstairs, she looked at his kitchen island, empty now. No flowers, no baked goods, no bowl of oranges or lemons. All traces of her, erased. She put a martini glass in the freezer...a reminder to relax and enjoy and indulge once in a while. He deserved that.

A knock at the door made her jump. She answered it, and there stood a woman about her own age, and Fluffina, on a leash, wagging her plumy tail.

"Hi!" said the woman. "You live here, right?"

"Um...not exactly, no. I was staying here for a while, but that's all done now." Again, her throat tightened.

"Oh. I'm Fiona? I live down the beach? Listen, I know this is completely stupid, but you like her, right?" She indicated the dog.

"Fluffina?"

"Bailey. I've seen you playing with her? On the beach?"

Fluffina was so not a Bailey. "Yeah, I've played with her. She's such a good girl." Fluffina wagged and smiled her doggy smile in affirmation, and Winnie smiled back at her.

"Yeah," Fiona agreed. "Here's the thing. She's a lot. She's so energetic, and she sheds constantly. I mean, I love her, but like, my house? It's always a wreck. I was wondering if you wanted her. She cost a lot. She's purebred and everything."

"You're giving her away because she sheds?" Winnie asked. Clearly, the woman was a Disney villain if that was the case.

Fiona sighed. "I have two kids under four. I don't know what we were thinking. I just can't give her the attention she needs." She began to cry. "It's not fair to the dog. I thought I'd try you, but if you can't take her, I'll bring her to a shelter or whatever."

"No! I mean, yes, I'll take her," Winnie said. "But I live in Wellfleet, not here, so you and your kids won't see her."

"I'll just tell the kids a nice lady owns her now. Will you take her to the beach? She loves running."

"I live right across the street from the water. Here, give me your phone number, and I'll text you pictures. You and the kids can even come visit if you want."

"Really? God, thank you. And like, you can stop by if you're down here, too. Seriously. Thank you."

A few minutes later, Fiona had given her a bag of food

from the car (she'd clearly assumed Winnie would say yes), some squeaky toys and a dog bed covered in a thick layer of white fur on it. "Bye, Bailey. I mean, Fluffina, you said?" She smiled at Winnie. "Good luck. Thanks again."

The dog's tail wagged as Fiona walked away, but otherwise, she didn't seem at all sad. "Well, then, Fluffina," Winnie said, and the dog looked at her, eyes bright and excited. "Who wants to go for a ride?"

TWENTY-TWO

LORENZO

In the weeks since he'd fired Winnie, Lorenzo's life went along in an uninterrupted, seamless fashion. The cleaning staff came and went with only a text notification that they had been there. The landscapers cleaned up after a Thanksgiving nor'easter before he was even aware of how hard the storm had hit. He received emails saying his various bills had been paid automatically, something Winnie had set up during her tenure. In Boston, his dry cleaning and laundry were picked up and delivered, neatly folded or hanging in biodegradable plastic, waiting in the foyer of his building with the doorman. Groceries appeared in refrigerated bags at the promised times. He received a notification that his Lamborghini had been detailed at his home in Chatham. And each night when he arrived home, either in Boston or Chatham, the lights were glowing warmly, thanks to a daylight sensor. Almost like someone was home.

Seamless and sterile. No flowers, no unrequested baked goods, no holiday décor or insouciant notes.

Which was fine, of course. He preferred it this way.

A colleague asked him to come to Mount Sinai in New

York to guest lecture her residents and scrub in on a delicate surgery. Lorenzo made his own hotel and train reservations without issue. The train was on time. The hotel manager at The Carlyle welcomed him back, and the suite was as nice as Lorenzo remembered. He ate dinner alone in the bar—a salad with grilled chicken. No drink, no dessert, no conversation. At Mt. Sinai the next day, the residents watched in reverence as he and Dr. Lad performed a multivisceral resection. Afterward, the younger doctors asked intelligent, respectful questions. He and Dr. Lad had a pleasant dinner together. His travel back to Boston the next day was uneventful, and he worked on the train.

His orderly life was like a vast white tunnel, silent and immaculate, the memory of little flashes of color and noise reverberating around him. He found himself running along the Charles, a deviation from his regular course, his steps slowing near Fiedler Dock.

He managed to dodge his family at Thanksgiving by covering trauma surgery for the weekend at Mass General. The following Friday evening, he drove down to Chatham. No traffic at the bridge, smooth sailing on Route 6.

On his front steps sat an insulated bag of groceries and two flower arrangements. Right. In a moment of weakness yesterday, after the bowel resection and before the laparotomy for the septic abdomen, he'd gone online and ordered two flower arrangements. Why? Because he missed having flowers in the house. Now, staring at them, he felt ridiculous. They looked forced and fake, like the flowers for an elderly aunt's funeral. They were well-intentioned, but stiff and off the mark.

Just like he was.

With a sigh, he left them there and went inside. The house was cold since he'd forgotten to turn on the heat via the app Winnie had downloaded. He tapped the thermostats, heard the low hum of the furnace, and wandered through the house, adjusting the lights.

Once, it had been a relief to come here to pristine, sleek silence, knowing the house would be exactly as he'd left it. Now, he felt as if he was living in a staged model home. He paused at the picture of himself meeting William for the first time, the infant staring straight into his eyes. He'd felt such a rush of connection to the baby, his sister's firstborn. His beautiful, kindhearted sister had become a mother, and this perfect little child had made him an uncle. He'd always imagined that his siblings would procreate, but he had not expected the intensity of his new role, like a flash-fire in his chest. William had made him an *uncle*. An eight-pound baby had looked up at him with complete trust and love, gazing back at him in wonder, and suddenly, Lorenzo was someone entirely new, something he had never been before.

Now, the same child was terrified at the sight of him.

That moment with Winnie in the elevator at the Mark Hopkins Hotel, he'd felt the same way—new. Full of potential, about to start something incredible. She *saw* him. And God, she was...everything. Fierce. Wise. Subtle and sharp, and funny. Brave. She took down her former lover in that airport without a single thought for how she might seem, who might be watching or listening, or judging. When that little boy was floating off into the Charles, she'd known exactly what to do, and because of her, Lorenzo had been able to hang onto the boy while she got them both to safety.

Had he actually told her she was an underachiever?

God, he'd fucked things up.

Lorenzo knew he was on some sort of spectrum, both because of biology and his upbringing and, at some point, choice. Medicine, the human anatomy, the miracles of science were clearer and more beautiful without the clouds of emotion. If he looked at a hemorrhaging pancreas, he needed to think about repairing the splenic artery, not about the fact that the patient was the mother of three and the victim of a hate crime.

It had always served him well professionally, this lack of emotion. But lately...since Winnie, damn her...he didn't feel well-served at all.

The vast darkness of sea beyond his yard was inky tonight, not a star to be seen. If he went outside and walked on the beach, he'd see the glimmer of lights in other houses along the shore and hear the shushing of the ocean. The thought made him feel unbearably lonely.

He wished he could get a dog. It just wasn't practical for someone with his schedule. Maybe a turtle, then.

He shook off the melancholy. This place was his escape, his time off after ten days solid of surgeries and teaching. He unloaded the groceries—fresh produce and fish—but was not inspired to make anything. Got out the bottle of Brennevin. He should've chilled the glass. He opened the freezer to stick one in, only to find one already there.

There she was again.

He took it out and poured himself a splash. Found himself wandering down the hallway to the stairs, then into the family room where Winnie had chosen the couch. He walked past it, looked into her room. It smelled clean and fresh, with maybe a hint of Ivory soap.

He went back and sat on the red velvet sofa. It was very comfortable. Another sip of Brennevin, its sharp, spicy flavor familiar and pleasing. He would not be depressed. He was a successful man, relaxing in his beautiful home. He had everything.

He picked up the remote control and turned on the TV.

A football game was on. He sat for a minute or two, calculating the brain damage each player was sustaining through each helmet-to-helmet crash. Humans were so fragile. Stupid, too, to risk brain function for a sport that might support them for a few years. Nevertheless, he admired a particularly clever block and the long pass the quarterback then threw.

Well. Not really his thing. A movie? Again, not really him. A documentary, then. Or nothing. There was a new reference manual on robotic and computer-assisted surgery. Or he could reread *The Emperor of All Maladies* for fun.

There was a joke in that last line. He wished someone were here to say it.

The house ticked and hummed around him, and he found himself listening for footsteps or a voice.

He did not appreciate feeling lonely in his own house.

And suddenly, there *was* noise upstairs. Sibling noise. "Lorenzo? You home, brother?"

He went up to find Dante and their sisters in his kitchen, pizza boxes stacked on the island. Dante was stashing beer in the fridge. No spouses, no kids. "Hi there!" Sofia said, giving him a hug. "We thought we'd bring you some unhealthy food, since you missed Thanksgiving."

Isabella hugged him too. "Sorry you had to work last weekend, pal," she said. "We missed you."

"Beer?" Dante asked, holding up a can.

"No, thanks," Lorenzo said, indicating his own glass. Then he set that down and said, "Actually, sure. Thanks. How was Thanksgiving?"

The three exchanged amused looks. "You know how it is," Izzy said. "Mom in a state of near panic, Dad getting in the way, Aunt Barb telling Mom her stuffing needs salt,

Uncle Lou asleep in front of the game before we even sat down."

"William had a tantrum because I wouldn't let him have a bite of the sponge," Sofia added. "Cried so hard he threw up on Lark, who then also threw up."

"But in a trash can, and beautifully," Dante said.

Before Lorenzo knew it, Sofia had gotten out plates, Izzy had grabbed glasses and a bottle of pinot noir, and Dante was patting the chair next to him.

It occurred to Lorenzo that he and his siblings had not eaten a meal, just the four of them, ever.

"This is the first time we've done this," he said, then regretted the comment.

"I think it is," Dante said. "At least, as adults. When we were little and you were home, Lorenzo, Mom and Dad would go out for a movie once in a while."

A memory stirred. Yes. That was true. He'd been put in charge occasionally. And because the other three were eating already, he took a bite of greasy pizza. God, it was good, and so, so bad for them.

"Remember the time Izzy cut her hand?" Dante continued. "She broke a glass and sliced herself pretty good."

Lorenzo did remember. He'd been fourteen at the time, unable to drive his sister to the ER. He'd wanted to stitch her up, but of course, his parents didn't have a suture kit, so he'd improvised Steri-Strips with gauze and painter's tape. By the time their parents had gotten home (it hadn't been a 911 type of emergency, he had decided), the bleeding had stopped.

"Oh, my God, I cried so hard," Sofia said. "A lot harder than you, Izzy."

"Yeah. Then you fainted and stole my thunder," Izzy said. "And you, Dante, couldn't stop laughing at Sofia. But at least I had a proper big brother to take care of me," Izzy said. "I was probably your first patient, Lorenzo."

"Pretty sure *I* was his first patient," Dante said. "I was, I don't know, three? Scraped my chin, and for some reason, I went to Lorenzo instead of Mom or Dad, and you put a Band-Aid on me." He paused. "It's one of my first memories, actually."

Lorenzo remembered that one, too. His brother's big brown eyes so trusting as Lorenzo held the wet face cloth against his chin. Dante had clutched Lorenzo's shirt in one fist, the tears sliding silently down his cute little face. And then, when the scrape was bandaged, Lorenzo had kissed his little brother's forehead and told him he was brave.

He hadn't thought about that in decades. There was an abrupt stinging behind his eyes.

"I used to go into your bedroom and watch you sleep, Lorenzo," Sofia said, her voice gentle. "It felt like Christmas whenever you were there."

"I think I learned to count by asking Mom how many days till you'd be home," Izzy said, covering Lorenzo's hand with hers.

"And I cried every time you went back," Dante said. "Stood at the window and bawled till I couldn't see the car anymore. So I guess what we're all saying, brother, is that we missed you, too. We knew you were smarter than the rest of us combined—"

"I take offense at that, yet admit that it's true," Izzy said.

"—and we were all a little in awe of you," Dante finished. "Which is not to say you haven't been a dick at times, of course. But we're so proud of you, Lorenzo. Not because of the houses and the money and all that, which is great, of course. But because you did something amazing with what you had."

"Exactly," Izzy said. "Of course you're freakishly smart. But you also worked your ass off. Mom and Dad still feel guilty about St. George's, and Mom had a point. It was a damned if you do, damned if you don't situation. Keep the wunderkind home in a plain old public school, or send you somewhere where your brain would be fed the superfood it needed. They wanted the best for you, and here you are. The best." She paused. "Sorry I was so bitchy at dinner when you were trying to talk."

"You're one of us, Lorenzo," Sofia said. "You always have been. I'm sorry if we've made you feel any other way. We adore you, big brother."

"True story," Dante said.

And Lorenzo Santini, the guy with all the letters and titles after his name, would have answered, but he couldn't, because apparently, he was crying, and then his sisters and brother patted and hugged and smacked him and told him to eat his pizza and drink his beer.

And so he did.

TWENTY-THREE

WINNIE

On the morning of December twelfth, Winnie woke up to a snowstorm, crashing waves, and a cold nose in her ear. "You want to go out?" she asked Fluffina. Fluffina did. She always did. After a romp on the beach, many sticks fetched, a brisk toweling off, brushing and breakfast, Winnie told Fluffina to be a good girl for Destiny, who would come over later to walk her. "I love you," she said, kissing the dog on the head. "See you tonight." Then she drove down to the Chatham Bars Inn to do her thing and marry off her brother.

Rosie declared the weather "magical." She and the Smith family females were in a cottage getting hair and makeup done. Rosie was relaxed and happy, and literally glowing. "You go hang with the boys," she told Winnie. "I'll give you a shout if I need anything, but I think we're all set."

"I'm proud to have you as a sister," Winnie said, giving her a hug. "Don't tell the others, but you're already my favorite."

"I heard that," Lark and Addie said in unison, and Harlow laughed.

Outside, the wind howled, and Winnie bent her head as

she walked to the hotel proper. Robbie and the other guys were in the presidential suite, all looking very handsome. The ocean roared its wintry howl, and the wind bent the pine trees. "Lucky weather," Winnie said. "It's so you, Robbie." And it was. Attention grabbing and romantic, just like Robbie.

"Winnie! You look beautiful! What a happy day!" Grandpop said, adjusting his bowtie. "You'll be glad to know I've whittled my speech down to twenty-two minutes."

"Hey, Aunt Winnie. Heard you got a dog. Is she here?" Matthew asked. Winnie swore he'd gotten taller since the summer.

"You'll have to visit me tomorrow to meet her," Winnie said. "You look wicked handsome, honey." He was a groomsman, too. The men wore tuxedos, and Winnie wore a long black dress with a boat neckline and low back, scored with Destiny's help from ThredUp.

"Austin, no shots," Winnie said. Then her parents came in, and Mom started crying at the sight (and relief, no doubt) of her baby in a tux. Winnie instructed the photographer to get the right pictures—Mom pinning on Robbie's boutonniere; Dad, Grandpop, Robbie and Matthew, the four generations; her and Robbie together, just the two of them. "In honor of us sharing a room for eight years and not killing each other," she said.

"You clean up nice, Windmill," Robbie said. "Some people might even say you're pretty, but I'm not one of them."

"Some people *are* saying you're totally out of your league with Rosie," Winnie said. "Which we all know is true."

"Amen to that," Robbie said. "Matthew, get in here,

buddy. I want a picture of just the two of us. Damn, we look like twins."

"Twins if Matthew had spent too many years drinking too many beers, smoking too much weed and not believing in sunscreen," Winnie said. But yes. Their nephew looked so much like Robbie they could be brothers.

"You're my cautionary tale," Matthew said, grinning. "Fifty-factor for life."

Winnie looked at her phone. "Time to get you married off before Rosie wakes up from her fever dream," she said.

The inn sparkled with fairy lights, and dozens of white and velvety red wedding flower arrangements added luscious pops of color. Rosie's dress was all lace, making her look like a frost princess, and her attendants—Harlow as woman of honor, Lark and Addie and Lorelei, a more recent friend—wore crimson. Esme, Imogen and Luna all wore white tulle dresses with crimson satin bows, and Mr. Wolfe cried as he walked his only child down the aisle. Robbie wiped his eyes, hugged Victor and told Rosie she was beautiful, his voice breaking.

Like most weddings, it was happy and meaningful, Winnie thought. Personally, she'd elope if the day ever came, then let her family know a month or so later. But her eyes were wet as her brother read the surprisingly lovely and solemn vows he had written himself. In the front row, her mom wiped her eyes, and Dad put his arm around her, while Esme and Imogen wrestled off to one side. Rosie cried through her own vows, and as Grandpop handed them their rings, there wasn't a dry eye in the house.

Then Robbie was told to kiss his bride, which he did with great enthusiasm, and everyone cheered. Winnie took Grandpop's arm and they followed the couple down the aisle toward the cocktail and mocktail hour.

"I hope to see you get married, too, someday," Grandpop said, squeezing her a little closer.

"I like being a spinster," she said. "It suits me."

"Well, then. If you're happy, your ancient grandfather is happy. And I'm excited to be your first official client! Perhaps we'll finally find my phone."

"Which one?" Somewhere in Grandpop's rambling, charming house behind the bookstore lived at least five missing iPhones.

Winnie was once again starting her own business—Scarlet Woman Home and Office Organization. After an evening spent with her sisters, mom and Rosie brainstorming names, she decided that Winnie Smith was just not punchy enough for a business name. This one, they all agreed, would get people's attention. After helping Lorenzo, then his neighbor Joyce in Boston, Winnie felt like she'd finally found the career she was born to do. She was already enrolled in an online class for professional organizers and had joined the national association. Her parents had also lined her up for the new year, since they were selling the family home and downsizing.

Blakelee Johnson, mother of Nycholiss, Kaedeigh and elynne, had also hired her, about an hour after Winnie had posted her new business venture on the Wellfleet Facebook page. Blakelee was getting a divorce, finally, and Winnie gave her a 25% discount. She thought she'd make it a policy —if your partner's infidelity was the cause of your need for professional organizing, you deserved a break.

At the reception, drinks were had, food was eaten, and the band welcomed everyone. Grandpop's speech, which Winnie had punctuated with a slideshow of Robbie and Rosie as children, then as a couple, was a roaring success.

Now that the dancing was in full swing, Winnie

watched in her role as both sister and event planner. Honestly, the hotel staff was more than competent. It was nice to just step back and observe, a faint smile on her face, a bigger one in her heart, sipping a glass of excellent wine, waving to a sibling or guest (God, Jeff Bridges looked good!). The inn was stunning, the wild wind and weather making it feel as if they were in a particularly beautiful snow globe. Most people were staying at the inn, so driving home was not a consideration.

"I heard you don't have a date for this event," said a voice just behind her.

The voice caused her to freeze for a second. She turned. "Satan. How are you?"

TWENTY-FOUR

LORENZO

Lorenzo hated big, happy events. Too many people, too loud, too much sensory input. Theoretically, he was glad that other people were having fun, laughing, talking, dancing, all those alien activities that weren't part of his regular life. Coming here had been a move made in haste and desperation...but he had known she'd be here, courtesy of a text from Robbie, and the inn was ten minutes from his house.

"I'm fine," he said, aware that it was his turn to speak. He looked at her dress. "You look very...appropriate." Beautiful. He should've said beautiful, but wouldn't that have sounded strange, coming from his mouth?

Maybe it was wishful thinking, but he thought she almost smiled. "I didn't see your name on the guest list," she said. "This is a surprise."

"I was invited, which wasn't necessary, but I RSVP'ed no. I...I just wanted to see you, that's all." His molars ached. Ah. He was clenching his jaw.

"And so you have." She gave a twirl, and the sight of her

skin, the swish of her dress, felt like an oddly welcome punch in the chest. "Anything else?"

"I owe you an apology. I said things that were...wrong."

"Underachieving, condescending and tone-deaf. Those things?"

"Yes. Sorry." A cardinal flitted past the window, and Lorenzo immediately thought that the bird was like Winnie—a flash of dazzling color in his gray life.

"Apology accepted."

"Really?"

"Yes." She smiled faintly, and his chest ached with feeling. With fear...and hope.

His turn for words again. May as well get it over with. "I'm fairly sure I'm in love with you. It's awkward and uncomfortable, and I'm not sure how to handle it."

"That's so romantic, Lorenzo. Wow."

"Romantic is not really in my wheelhouse."

"No."

They looked at each other for a minute, then Robbie skidded up, literally sliding into her. "Hey, man! Glad you came! Are you here to beg my sister to marry you? That would be fine with me, just saying."

Lorenzo looked at him. "No," he said. "Congratulations, by the way."

"Thanks! I'm a lucky man. Sorry, Winnipeg. I tried." He grinned and darted off again.

"I might be here to beg you to date me, though," Lorenzo said. "I...well. As I said, I miss you. My life seems very...gray these days. Without you in it, that is."

Her face didn't move, but her lovely eyes softened, and it occurred to Lorenzo that she was the most beautiful woman in this room, and if he couldn't ever touch her hair or feel her skin or kiss her or hear her laugh, his life would be very long and bleak.

"Okay," she said.

"Okay?"

"Okay, I'll date you. I'm fairly sure I'm in love with you, too." Then she stood on her tiptoes, put a hand over his thudding heart, and kissed him chastely on the lips.

"Oh, huzzah!" came a voice. Robert Smith, the grandfather. "Young man, I was *hoping* you'd fall for my granddaughter! I had a sense when we were at that strip club! I asked myself, 'Do you know who would be perfect for Winnie? This young man right here.' And I was right! Now, don't tell the others this, but she's my favorite."

"Grandpop, you said literally the same thing to me ten seconds ago," said Winnie's sister. The bookstore sister. "Winnie, I'm his favorite, but I agree with everything else he just said. Grandpop, come dance with us, okay? Talk to you later." She smiled at Lorenzo and led the old man away.

"Would you like to dance?" Lorenzo asked, his hand aching to touch the bare skin on Winnie's back.

"Not really," she said, "but in your case, I'll make an exception."

He took her in his arms, skimmed his fingertips along her spine and felt her shiver. Suddenly, he felt *right*. That was not a feeling he had often, other than when he was operating on someone, but certainty enveloped him in a warm embrace.

"I have a dog now," she said, then cleared her throat, and it occurred to him that she was feeling a lot of things, too.

"I like dogs."

"She sheds a lot."

"There are machines for that, aren't there?"

"There are. I just ordered a Roomba."

"You look so beautiful," he said, letting his lips brush her ear.

"There you go," she whispered a little breathlessly. "Well done."

He held her a little closer, breathed in her clean, soft smell—Ivory soap and honey—and closed his eyes. "Is it too early to propose?" he murmured.

"Yes," she said, pulling back to look into his eyes. "But hold that thought and ask again in a few months."

He would. He would put a note in his calendar, and in the spring when the flowers were blooming and the air was soft, he would ask Windsor Smith to marry him.

If he wasn't mistaken—and really, he hardly ever was—she would say yes.

THE END

THANK you for reading *Once in a Blue Moon*. This novella was a labor of love and gift to my loyal readers. I hope you enjoyed seeing Dr. Satan and Winnie get their happy ending! If you liked the book and felt like leaving a review on Amazon or Goodreads, I surely would appreciate it!

Don't forget to sign up for my newsletters, which cover my life as an author, books I love, family life and some of the funnier things that happen to me, like almost dying in hot yoga, or why I'm not allowed to get pedicures anymore. I'll also make sure you never miss a new release or sale. Sign up at kristanhiggins.com.

If you want to keep reading about the Smith family and

other residents of Wellfleet, Massachusetts, make sure you check out these three books:

Out of the Clear Blue Sky

When Lillie Silva finds herself the victim of her husband's midlife crisis, she makes a decision: she will make her husband pay, whether it's leaving him an unexpected housewarming gift in the form of a skunk or crashing his wedding. But as the months pass, she finds that there's more to her than wife, mother and midwife, and the best may well be just around the corner. Start reading Out of the Clear Blue Sky now.

Start Reading Out of the Clear Blue Sky Now

A Little Ray of Sunshine

Harlow thought her past was neatly tucked away—until her secret son shows up in her bookstore. As Matthew reunites with his birth mother and blindsides his adoptive parents, two families collide in one unforgettable Cape Cod summer that redefines love, motherhood and second chances.

Start Reading A Little Ray of Sunshine Now

Look on the Bright Side

Lark Smith had a plan: perfect marriage, thriving oncology career, happy family—then everything falls apart.
A fake relationship with gruff surgeon Lorenzo Santini promises solutions, but a seaside summer filled with unexpected love and unlikely friendships changes everything she thought she wanted.

Start Reading Look on the Bright Side Now

ACKNOWLEDGMENTS

The main characters in this book exchanged a couple of irritable sentences in *Look on the Bright Side,* and there it was. Without me planning it, a romance was born, and the savvy reader spotted it immediately. To everyone who wrote to ask when Winnie and Dr. Satan would have their own book, know that I heard you and was already on it.

To Shaunee Cole, who edited the story, and Gail Chianese, who proofread it, thank you for your care and thoughtfulness. How wonderful to have friends with such relevant skills! Thank you to Catherine Arendt, Joss Dey and Hilary Higgins Murray for brainstorming scenes with me (the bachelor party is a special favorite); and to Jamie Beck and the MTBs for the weekend in Vermont—Harper Ross, Jamie K. Schmidt, Regina Kyle, Gail Chianese, Jane Haertel, Megan Ryder.

Mel Jolly, we both know this book would've stayed on my computer were it not for you. Thank for doing everything necessary to get Winnie and Satan out in the world, Number One. Don't know how I'd do this job without you.

Thanks to my agent, Christina Hogrebe, for shepherding the audiobook into existence, and to the wonderful folks at Recorded Books.

To my lovely, fun, wonderful family—Terence, Declan, Flannery, Mike, the Peeper, the Butterfly, Hilary, Jackie, Huckleberry and Buttercup—I love you all more than I could ever say. You already know this, but it bears repeating.

ALSO BY KRISTAN HIGGINS

The Wellfleet Novels*

Look on the Bright Side

A Little Ray of Sunshine

Out of the Clear Blue Sky

Pack Up the Moon

The Stoningham Novels*

Always the Last to Know

Life and Other Inconveniences

The Cambry-on-Hudson Novels*

Good Luck with That

On Second Thought

If You Only Knew

The Blue Heron Series

The Best Man

The Perfect Match

Waiting on You

In Your Dreams

Anything for You

The Gideon's Cove Novels*

Catch of the Day

The Next Best Thing

Somebody to Love

Stand-Alone Novels

Pack Up the Moon

Now That You Mention It

Until There Was You

My One and Only

All I Ever Wanted

Too Good to Be True

Just One of the Guys

Fools Rush In

*These books are connected by location and crossover characters,
but are not considered a series.*

Visit my website at www.kristanhiggins.com and find my links to
social media, where I do my best to keep you entertained and
hopeful.